TANGLED LOVE

TANGLED BOOK ONE

AASKA SHAH

To the one who was my first love—thank you for teaching me that love can be both gentle and powerful. You'll always hold a special place in my heart.

To my parents, for their unwavering support, love, and belief in me. Your encouragement has been my greatest strength, and I am forever grateful.

To my friends, whose laughter, honesty, and presence have made every moment brighter. You've made life a journey worth living, and I can never thank you enough.

To everyone who believes in the magic of love, friendship, and the beauty of untold stories.

This book is for those who have ever felt tangled in their emotions, for those who have loved, lost, and learned.

Contents

Contents

Contents

Foreword

Every story begins with a spark—a moment, a feeling, or an experience that lingers in the heart long after it.

There's a magic in love that's hard to define—a deep, unspoken connection that pulls two souls together, no matter the obstacles. Tangled Love is a story about that kind of love, one that isn't always easy or perfect, but is real and raw, with all its twists and turns. It's about the moments when you are at your most vulnerable, when you fall in love without realizing it, and when the world around you seems to shift because of that one person.

In this first book of the Tangled series, we meet Rishi and Aarna, two individuals whose paths cross from childhood, only to intertwine in ways they never expected. Their story is one of growth, friendship, misunderstandings, and the undeniable pull of affection that neither can ignore. Through their ups and downs, their love for each other takes shape, and with it, they begin to understand not only each other but themselves as well.

As you read, you'll find yourself entangled in their emotions—whether it's the giddy excitement of first love, the pain of heartache, or the bittersweet realization that love often comes with its own set of complications. But, like any love story worth telling, it's a journey that is far from over.

I invite you to join Rishi and Aarna as they navigate the beautiful mess of growing up, discovering who they are, and figuring out how to love, both themselves and each other. This book isn't just about romance—it's about friendship, trust, and the emotional tangle that we all face in life.

Welcome to Tangled Love. I hope you find yourself just as captivated by their journey as I was in writing it.

— Aaska

Preface

The idea for this story was born from a place of nostalgia—of remembering the first time I ever truly felt the intense, all-consuming rush of a crush, the excitement and fear that come with discovering love, and the bittersweet realization that it's never as simple as we want it to be.

Like many of us, I remember my school days as a whirlwind of emotions, lessons, and unforgettable moments. But there was one memory that always stayed with me: my first love. It wasn't a grand, dramatic romance—it was awkward, subtle, and full of unspoken words. And yet, it left a mark that shaped the way I would view love, relationships, and friendship for years to come.

This book is a reflection of that time, that feeling, and the way we grow up alongside the people who shape us. The characters you'll meet in this story—Aarna and Rishi—are, in many ways, versions of who I was at that age. They struggle with the same insecurities, the same questions, and the same unvoiced hopes that I once did. Through them, I wanted to explore how love isn't always about grand gestures or perfect moments. Sometimes, it's in the quiet exchange of glances, the hesitant words, and the growth that happens when two people just click without even fully realizing it.

This story also touches on something I hold dear: the importance of friendships. Aarna and Rishi's journey doesn't just revolve around their evolving feelings for one another, but also the way their friendships influence them, challenge them, and help them grow. I think many of us can relate to the way our friendships shape our understanding of ourselves and the people we love.

Writing this book was not only a way to relive those memories but to capture the complexity of first loves and all the emotions that come with them—excitement, confusion, jealousy, and, ultimately, growth. It's a story for anyone who's ever had a crush, ever wondered whether someone feels the same, or ever wished they could turn back time and have the courage to speak their heart.

As you read Aarna and Rishi's story, I hope it brings you back to your own memories of young love and reminds you of the power of those first connections, the way they can change us, challenge us, and leave us with something we'll never forget.

Thank you for letting me share this journey with you.

Acknowledgements

First and foremost, I want to express my deepest gratitude to my readers—without your support and belief in my work, this book would not have been possible. Thank you for being a part of this journey, and for embracing the characters and their stories with open hearts.

To my family, your love and encouragement have been a constant source of strength. To my parents, thank you for always believing in me, even on days when I doubted myself. Your unwavering support has shaped me into who I am today.

A special thank you to my friends who have been my biggest cheerleaders. Your words of motivation and your ability to make me laugh when I needed it the most were invaluable. I couldn't have done this without you.

To my editor, thank you for your patience, your attention to detail, and for guiding me to make Tangled Love the best version of itself. Your insight was instrumental in bringing this story to life.

To the countless authors whose books inspired me—thank you for showing me what's possible when you pour your heart and soul into a story. Your work continues to fuel my own passion for writing.

To anyone who has ever loved, lost, or experienced the thrill of young love—this book is for you. And lastly, thank you to my readers. You are the reason I write. I hope this story resonates with you, and I'm grateful to share it with you.

Prologue

Love, they say, is the most unpredictable force in the world—wild, untamed, and, at times, tangled beyond recognition. But no one tells you that sometimes, it's also messy, heartbreaking, and hard to let go of, even when you should.

Aarna never expected it. She was the calm, composed one, the girl who always focused on her studies and dreamed of a future where everything would fall into place. But life doesn't always follow the plans we make. Sometimes, it throws unexpected love into the mix, forcing us to face feelings we didn't know existed and dreams we didn't know we had.

Rishi, on the other hand, had never believed in love. It seemed like something other people got caught up in, a beautiful distraction from reality. Until, one day, it wasn't. Until one day, Aarna came into his life, and everything shifted.

It wasn't instant. It wasn't perfect. It wasn't easy. But it was real. And as they navigated their friendship, their feelings, and the complications of life, they learned that love doesn't always fit into a neat little box. Sometimes, it's tangled.

This is the beginning of their story. A story of growth, heartache, and rediscovery. Of friendship that becomes something more, and love that grows, even when it feels impossible. Tangled Love is where it all starts.

And, like all tangled stories, there's no clear path. Just two people trying to find their way to each other, through all the twists and turns that life throws at them.

It's not just a love story. It's a journey. One that will take them through heartbreak, joy, confusion, and hope, all wrapped in the beautiful mess of growing up.

This is their story.

This is Tangled Love.

1

AARNA

Her name, like her presence, carried an aura of quiet elegance. Calm and composed, she had an innate ability to steady any storm, whether it was an argument among friends or the chaos of her own emotions. She wasn't one to lose her temper often; instead, she approached life with a sense of balance, always weighing her words and actions carefully.

Honesty was her defining trait. She couldn't lie to save her life, which often made her endearingly transparent. You could see every emotion she felt—joy, frustration, or heartbreak—right there in her eyes, even when her lips didn't utter a word.

Aarna had always been studious. She wasn't just someone who excelled academically; she genuinely loved the process of learning. Books were her constant companions, her escape, her solace. Whether it was a complex accounting problem or a historical event she was reading about, she absorbed it all with enthusiasm.

Her dreams were big but grounded. While others around her floated on fleeting whims, Aarna planned every step of her journey meticulously. She wanted to become a Chartered Accountant, a goal that reflected not only her intellect but also her determination.

But beneath her composed exterior lay a heart that longed for something more. Aarna believed in true love—the kind of love that was patient, unwavering, and timeless. She had seen glimpses of it in stories, in the quiet moments of her favorite books, and in the way some people looked at each other with unspoken understanding. She knew, deep in her heart, that one day, love would find her. And when it did, it would be as real and honest as she was.

Despite her quiet demeanor, there was something undeniably magnetic about her. Maybe it was the way her laughter, rare but heartfelt, lit up the room. Or perhaps it was her ability to listen, really listen, making you feel like the most important person in the world.

Aarna was the kind of person you couldn't help but admire, the kind of person who made you believe in the beauty of sincerity, hard work, and quiet resilience. Calm, composed, honest, studious, and a true romantic at heart. Above all, she was real.

She was Aarna.

2

RISHI

Rishi.

There was something effortlessly captivating about him—a charm that didn't rely on loud words or extravagant gestures. Rishi had his own way of drawing people in, whether it was through his quick wit, his playful teasing, or the way his eyes lit up when he talked about the things he loved.

And one of those loves was football. Rishi wasn't just good at it; he was passionate. The thrill of the game, the rush of a perfectly executed goal, the camaraderie with his teammates—it all made him feel alive. On the field, he was focused and driven, almost like he became a different person, someone unstoppable.

Off the field, though, Rishi wasn't always as energetic. He had a lazy streak that often got him into trouble. Whether it was procrastinating on homework or sleeping through his alarm, he had a knack for pushing the limits of how late he could be without getting into serious trouble. But somehow, his charm always bailed him out.

Another of Rishi's passions was art. His room was filled with sketches and paintings, each one a glimpse into the way he saw the world. He could spend hours with a pencil in hand, shading in the details of a landscape or capturing the raw emotion in a pair of eyes. Art was his escape, his way of expressing what words couldn't.

Rishi had always been the type to scoff at the idea of love. To him, it was just a fleeting emotion, something people romanticized but rarely experienced in its truest form. Or so he thought—until it happened to him. When love did find him, it came unexpectedly, like a quiet knock on the door he didn't even know was there. And when he opened that door, everything he believed about love changed.

He wasn't perfect, and he didn't try to be. He made mistakes, sometimes big ones, but he always tried to make up for them. There was a depth to Rishi, a complexity that made him hard to define. Charming yet lazy, passionate yet skeptical, artistic yet grounded.

Rishi was someone who made you feel like life was an adventure worth taking—messy, unpredictable, and undeniably beautiful.

He was Rishi.

3
A NEW BEGINNING

AARNA

December 25th, 2016.

It was a cold day in Mumbai, colder than I ever remembered, as though the city itself had decided to dress in winter just for Christmas. I was eleven, standing at the threshold of childhood, unaware that a single moment would mark the beginning of something I couldn't yet understand.

Christmas had always been my favorite holiday, and for good reason. It was more than the carols, the presents, or the twinkling lights. It was a time for reflection, for family, for the kind of joy that settled deep in your heart and warmed you from the inside. I loved everything about Christmas—especially the hot chocolate. The rich, steaming cup in my hands that day felt like it could melt away any worry... and little did I know, I would need it more than ever.

That day, I was at Canopy Mall with my family. It was the usual Christmas routine: Mom was lost in the endless racks of clothes, Dad was glued to his phone for yet another business call, and my younger sister, Kaina, was happily lost in the world of Barbies with her caretaker. I was on my own, wandering aimlessly through my favorite candy store, when something shifted in the air around me.

I could feel it—like a sudden pull in my chest, an odd flutter in my stomach. It was strange. My heart began to beat faster, and my skin tingled with something I couldn't name. I didn't understand it at first. Was it the cold? Was it the Christmas lights making everything feel magical?

But no... it was him.

Behind me, I heard a familiar voice—one that had echoed through my childhood, one that had always been a source of comfort. Rishi. My childhood friend. The boy who had been a constant in my life since kindergarten. But today, something felt different. I'd seen him a thousand times, shared countless laughs, and even exchanged secrets with him like we were the best of friends. But that afternoon, I could feel his presence in a way I'd never felt before.

The mall suddenly seemed quieter, the buzz of holiday shoppers dimmed in comparison to the pounding of my heart. I turned to look at him, and the world felt like it paused, if only for a moment. His smile, so familiar, held something new in it—something that made the space between us feel more charged than ever.

Was I imagining it? Was this just the magic of Christmas playing tricks on me?

The day passed in a blur. We shared some candy, exchanged pleasantries with our parents, and eventually headed out for dinner. But I couldn't shake the feeling that something had changed, something I didn't quite understand yet.

Why did it feel like everything had changed in the span of a few hours? I tried to ignore it, to brush it off. It was just a holiday. Nothing more, nothing less. But deep down, I knew that I couldn't let go of that moment. I couldn't forget the way my heart had raced when he'd been near me.

Time passed. The year drifted by like a gentle tide, and before I knew it, I was stepping into grade 7. Everything was shifting. Puberty. Friendships. My sense of self. And with it, the growing awareness of feelings I couldn't control.

I found myself thinking about Rishi more than I ever had before. He was just a friend, wasn't he? But then again, why did every conversation with him now feel so much heavier? Why did I care so much about the sound of his laughter? Why did every touch, every glance, feel like it meant something more?

That Christmas day had been the start of something—something I wasn't yet ready for, something that would shake my world in ways I couldn't predict. I couldn't stop thinking about it, about him. Maybe it was a crush. Maybe it was something else. But deep down, I knew one thing for sure: I was standing at the edge of something that would change everything.

And I wasn't sure I was ready for it.

4

THE FIRST MEET

RISHI

She was wearing that pink cropped top and skirt, her ponytail bouncing like it always did, so effortlessly cute. But that day, something about her struck me. I'd seen Aarna a million times before—she had been my best friend for as long as I could remember. Our birthdays were only fifteen days apart, we went to the same dance classes, had the same Math tutor (who, by the way, she still struggled with)—we shared everything. We'd practically grown up together.

Yet there I was, standing a few feet away from her at Canopy Mall, feeling like I was seeing her for the first time. The Christmas lights flickered above, but they didn't shine nearly as brightly as her smile. Why was she so beautiful? I couldn't understand it. I'd seen her in every possible way—frustrating, annoying, silly—but never like this. Never like this. My chest tightened. Why was my heart racing?

Her eyes locked with mine for a brief second, and there it was again—the thing I couldn't quite place. It was like she was looking at me, but not really seeing me. As if I were a stranger she barely recognized. And the worst part? I was doing the same thing. Avoiding her gaze. Pretending like everything was fine when inside, it felt like I was drowning.

We used to be inseparable. I could never imagine a day without Aarna. But over the past year, we'd slowly drifted apart, and I had no idea why. I could barely talk to her at school. At dance class, we barely exchanged words. Even at family gatherings, we'd sit on opposite sides of the room, as though there was some invisible wall between us that neither of us could tear down.

And I hated it. I hated that we were like this now. She was still my best friend. I should've been able to talk to her about anything. But there was this strange, suffocating distance between us now. This unspoken thing that neither of us could admit.

I missed her. God, I missed her. I missed the way we used to laugh, the way we'd tease each other until we couldn't breathe. But most of all, I missed the way we used to feel about each other—so sure of our bond. It was gone. And I didn't know how to get it back.

I remember the moment I realized it for the first time—the moment I knew I had fallen for her. It was Diwali. She was wearing a light blue skirt, and her hair was loose around her shoulders, shining in the soft glow of the lights. The way she looked that day—it hit me like a tidal wave. I had feelings for Aarna. Real feelings. The kind of feelings I couldn't ignore anymore.

I had spent the whole year trying to push her away. I'd distanced myself, convinced myself that we were just friends—just friends. But when I saw her that day, something inside me snapped. I needed her. I wanted her. But how could I say that? How could I admit that to myself, let alone to her?

The year passed, and before I knew it, we were in grade 7. For the first time in our entire school lives, we were in the same division. It felt like fate—like something was pulling us back together—but it wasn't the reunion I'd imagined. It wasn't a happy, easy reunion. It felt like a confrontation. Like we were on the edge of something we didn't know how to navigate.

Then, it was her birthday. The day I couldn't ignore it any longer. She looked perfect—the same Aarna, but somehow... different. Older. Beautiful. She was no longer the little girl I'd grown up with. She was a girl I was falling for, and it terrified me.

I tried to act normal. I walked up to her, tried to keep my voice steady. "Happy birthday, Aarna. Do you want to go bowling today?"

She turned to me, her eyes almost flat, distant. "I've got other plans," she said. "Nia and Erika are coming over for games. You should join us, though. We can invite Aarush and Rohan, too."

I felt this sharp pang in my chest, but I hid it. I hid it. "Sure. Sounds good," I said, but the words felt hollow. My heart wasn't in it. I wasn't sure if it was ever going to be.

We were sitting on different sides of a chasm, and I didn't know how to bridge it. I wanted to scream at her, Tell me why we're like this now! I wanted to ask her what had happened, why she was pulling away, why it felt like she was slipping through my fingers.

But I didn't. I couldn't.

That day, I realized something I hadn't wanted to face: I had fallen in love with my best friend. And I had no idea what to do about it. How could I even tell her, when I wasn't sure she still saw me as anything more than just a friend?

I was afraid of losing her entirely, afraid that telling her how I felt would destroy everything between us. But I was also afraid of living with the silence, with the distance.

I didn't know which scared me more.

5

BUTTERFLIES

AARNA

Today was the day. The day I had been dreaming of, wishing for—practically praying for. Rishi was going to come over. Rishi. The one guy who had made my heart race since the day we met. The one who had always been my best friend... but somewhere along the way, something had changed. And now, here we were. My birthday. And he was actually coming over.

It was supposed to be the best birthday ever. The moment I had been waiting for, fantasizing about. The kind of moment you play out in your head a thousand times—where it's just the two of you, alone. Where you go bowling together, maybe grab some mac n' cheese at the diner, then sit in front of a screen and watch Minions or something silly. Just the two of you.

But instead, I was here, preparing for the birthday party with my friends. Nia, Erika, Aarush, and Rohan. The whole gang. The whole gang, except for him. Rishi.

I had to share him. I had to pretend like I wasn't dying to spend this entire day alone with him. I could already feel the nerves building in my chest as I thought about the way I'd have to divide my attention, talking to my friends, playing games, keeping up appearances. And all the while, he would be there, watching me, probably laughing with the others, but I'd be stuck with the nagging feeling that the one moment I really wanted—just us—was slipping through my fingers.

But at least he was here. He had asked to hang out with me. Rishi had never asked a girl to hang out like this. It wasn't like him. Not to mention, the girls at school had always been throwing themselves at him, and he had turned them down, time and time again. He had never looked at them the way he had looked at me that day at Canopy Mall. He'd never said, "Let's hang out, just us."

And that terrified me. Why now? After months of silence, of barely talking, why had he asked me? What had changed? I wanted to believe it was because he cared about me, that maybe he was feeling the same way I did. But then again, I couldn't be sure. Could I?

I wasn't even sure what to think about myself anymore. It had been a year since that day at Canopy Mall. A year since we had last shared that same space, that same unspoken connection. And since then? Everything had been different. We'd barely talked, barely looked at each other. So many things had changed between us—so many things I couldn't put into words.

But today... today felt like it could change everything. I hoped it would.

I stood in front of my mirror, the weight of my thoughts pressing down on me as I pulled on my green jumpsuit. Nia braided my hair for me—tight, precise, perfect. Nia was the kind of girl who never did anything halfway. Everything about her was carefully planned: her clothes, her makeup, her hair. Her life. She had this picture-perfect idea of how things should be, and I guess it rubbed off on me, in a way. Sometimes it frustrated me—the way everything had to be flawless, the way she controlled every little detail. But when you spend more than half your life with someone, you learn to adjust. I learned to live with her way, even if it made me feel a little less me sometimes.

As Nia finished the last braid, I looked at myself in the mirror. I was nervous. God, I was nervous. I didn't know what to expect today, what would happen, what he would say. What if this all blew up in my face? What if I was reading it wrong? What if he was just being polite, and I was reading too much into it?

I had to stop overthinking. I had to pull myself together. This was my birthday, after all.

But as soon as I stepped outside to welcome my friends, I saw him from the balcony, standing in the yard with the rest of the group. And everything inside me froze. I could feel my heartbeat in my throat. There he was. The guy who made my heart pound just by existing. He was wearing that stupidly handsome smile, talking to Aarush and Rohan—but my eyes couldn't leave him.

He was here. And everything inside me—every single feeling—flared to life all at once.

But was he really here for me? Or was he just here because he was being polite? Because it was my birthday and it was expected?

No. I couldn't think that way. I had to stop overthinking. I had to just enjoy the moment, whatever it was.

"Aarna, come on! You're getting late!" Nia's voice snapped me out of my thoughts.

I took a deep breath and walked outside, past my friends, my heart pounding in my chest like a drum. I couldn't stop the rush of emotions, but I had to hide it. I had to pretend like everything was fine, like I wasn't dying inside to know if he really felt the same.

I had to trust that, maybe today—just today—would be the start of something new. Something I had been hoping for, wishing for, for so long.

But what if... what if it wasn't?

6
THE GIFT

RISHI

She stepped into the room, and for a moment, everything slowed. A green jumpsuit, long earrings that caught the light just right, her hair braided perfectly—Aarna looked... incredible. She was always cute, always someone I could tease or joke around with, but today? Today, she was a different kind of beautiful. And for the first time, I noticed everything about her—the way the green fabric of her jumpsuit hugged her curves, how her earrings swayed with every movement, how her hair fell in soft waves around her shoulders.

It was almost maddening, how she had this effect on me now. But what hit me hardest was the band she was wearing on her wrist. It was the same one I had given her for her 9th birthday, a silly, cheap thing, but I remembered it perfectly. She probably didn't even remember it, but I did. I'd been thinking about that moment—thinking about how we used to be, how things had changed, how I had started feeling things for her I didn't understand.

I had a gift for her too, something I wasn't sure she'd even appreciate. My mom had chosen it—a keychain with a photo from our kindergarten days, when we were so carefree and innocent, when we didn't worry about anything except who could do the best cartwheel. It felt... cringe. Embarrassing, even. But I couldn't help it. I wanted to give her something that mattered. Something she'd keep with her for the years to come.

And as the others handed their gifts over—coupons for food, makeup, fancy skin products—my stomach twisted. What the hell was I doing here? I was giving her a keychain, and some other guy had given her a beautiful dress. I couldn't stand the thought of it. I knew exactly who had gifted her that dress—Sahel. The guy who followed Aarna around like a shadow, pretending like he was doing it casually, but I knew better. He'd always been there, lurking in the background, and now he was getting her this dress, just like that. I hated it. I hated that he was part of her life, that he was the one getting her things that were actually nice while I was here, clutching a silly little keychain.

But then—then I saw her face when she opened my gift. Her eyes widened as she looked at the keychain, and for a second, it was like time stood still. She blinked, and then—oh god—her eyes started to glisten, like she was holding back tears.

"Thank you," she mouthed, her voice barely above a whisper, and then—she shook my hand. My heart nearly stopped. Was she really that moved by something so simple, so... childish? She wasn't looking at me with the same distance that had been there for months. There was a warmth in her gaze, something softer, something that made my chest ache in the best and worst way.

She actually liked it.

It wasn't just a gift. It wasn't just some token she'd toss in a drawer and forget about. She was genuinely touched. She cared about it. She cared about me.

I could barely breathe. A wave of relief washed over me, and then, right on its heels, came the sinking feeling of want. I wanted more of her, all of her. I wanted her to remember this moment. To remember that it wasn't just a gift I gave her because it was her birthday—it was something I wanted her to cherish for the rest of her life. Something that would always make her think of me, no matter where we ended up. Not just a gift for today, or for the week, or the month.

I wanted her to remember us. To remember me.

But as I watched her smile and thank me, a thought gnawed at the back of my mind: What if that was all she ever saw me as? Just the guy who had been her best friend. The guy who handed over a gift that reminded her of when we were best friends. What if that was it?

And then, I looked over at Sahel, watching her with a kind of possessiveness in his eyes, and I couldn't help but feel a sharp stab of jealousy. I wanted to be the one who made her smile like that, the one who was the first person she turned to. I wanted her to see me like I was finally seeing her.

I knew I was playing with fire. But right then, I didn't care. I wanted her to remember me. To remember us.

For life.

7
A GIFT TO REMEMBER

AARNA

The day had been long, filled with the usual hustle of school, but I couldn't shake off the feeling that had settled in my chest. It was the gift Rishi had given me. That small, simple keychain with our picture from kindergarten. I had no words for how it made me feel. He had remembered, and somehow, that made all the difference. The memories flooded me in waves—those carefree days when we were just kids, sharing everything and not worrying about what was to come.

But now... everything was different.

I couldn't stop thinking about the way he had looked at me when he handed it to me. His eyes had held something—something I couldn't quite place. Was it affection? Was it just a gesture of friendship? Or was there something more?

I ran my fingers over the smooth surface of the keychain, my mind replaying the moments of the past few months. We had grown so close again, and yet... there was this distance, this tension I couldn't ignore. He was still Rishi—the same old friend who would tease me and laugh at my silly jokes—but there was something else there now. Something that made my heart race every time he was near.

I wanted to believe that maybe he felt the same way, that maybe he was confused just like me. But then, I thought about the way he laughed with Poorna, the way he talked to her, and a small pang of jealousy crept into my chest. Was I just another friend to him? Did he see me the way I saw him? Or had I been reading into things too much?

I closed my eyes, trying to calm my racing thoughts. Maybe I was overthinking. Maybe it was just a gift between friends—nothing more, nothing less. He had given me a keychain, not a declaration of his feelings. I had no right to expect more, right?

But then why did it hurt so much? Why did it feel like something was missing? Why did I feel this ache in my chest every time I saw him smile at someone else? Was it just me? Was I alone in this?

I looked at the keychain one more time, my thoughts tangled in a web of emotions I couldn't untangle. Maybe I was being foolish. Maybe I should just let it go, focus on school, and stop overthinking every little thing. After all, we were just friends, right?

But a small voice in my heart told me something different. Maybe, just maybe, I wasn't alone in these feelings. Maybe Rishi felt the same way.

But then, what if he didn't? What if this was just me, dreaming up something that wasn't real? I had to be honest with myself. I had to move on. I couldn't keep living in this limbo, holding onto a hope that might never come true.

So, for now, I made a decision. I would focus on my studies. I would stop thinking about Rishi and the things I couldn't have. I would bury these feelings deep down and pretend like they didn't exist. After all, what good was it to wish for something that might never be?

I placed the keychain in my drawer and closed it, my heart heavy but determined. It was time to move on. I couldn't keep waiting for something that wasn't meant to be.

8

TANGLED PATHS

RISHI

There was something about being around Aarna that always made me feel... right. She was like the missing piece I didn't even know I was searching for, like the air I breathed when I was drowning in the noise of everything else. Every time I was with her, it felt like I could finally be myself—no pretenses, no facades, just... us.

We'd spent so many years together, I never thought I'd feel this way. But now? Now it was different. I couldn't explain it. It wasn't just about the jokes we shared, or the way she would always get so serious about things that didn't even matter. It was something deeper. Every time I saw her smile, every time she'd roll her eyes at my lame jokes, every time she'd call me out for being a 'clueless idiot' (which I was, a lot of the time), it felt like home.

She had always been the person I could count on. She was my constant, my best friend. But somewhere along the way, something changed. I started wanting more. I didn't want to just be her best friend anymore. I wanted to be the person she turned to when she needed someone. I wanted to be the one she smiled at, the one who made her laugh, the one who'd stand by her side no matter what.

I didn't know how it happened or when it happened, but I was in love with Aarna. I knew it. And it terrified me.

I couldn't ignore it anymore. Every glance, every moment I spent with her, I realized that this was no longer about just friendship. It was about something more. Something that was scary and uncertain, but something that felt... real. And I couldn't stop it.

But she was... different now. I couldn't quite put my finger on it, but there was a distance between us. Aarna wasn't the same person I had always known. She wasn't as open with me anymore. I'd try to talk to her, make her laugh, but she was distracted, distant. She wasn't the Aarna who used to confide in me, who'd get into trouble with me over silly things. Now, she seemed focused on something else. And it stung, more than I wanted to admit.

I couldn't help but notice how she'd look at Poorna sometimes. How she would watch her, almost... studying her. It was like she was always comparing herself to Poorna, trying to measure up in ways that I didn't understand. I'd catch her glancing at me when I was with Poorna, like she was waiting for something, but never saying anything. It made my chest tighten.

Was she jealous?

The thought made me uncomfortable. But it didn't make sense. I wasn't interested in Poorna. Not like that.

I was interested in Aarna. Only Aarna.

But it felt like Aarna didn't see that. She was pulling away, and I didn't know why. I wanted to ask her, to just say something, but the words never came out right. Instead, I found myself trying to be around her in the little moments, trying to make her laugh, trying to remind her of how easy it was when we were just... us.

During lunch, I'd hang around her table, even when I wasn't part of the group. I'd sit with her and Nia, Aarush, and Rohan, pretending like I wasn't trying to stay close to her. But I was. Every time I caught her eyes, I'd feel this rush in my chest. Like we shared something unspoken.

When I saw her smile, even if it wasn't for me, it felt like I could breathe again. And when she ignored me? It was like a punch in the gut. I'd sit there, watching her laugh with someone else, pretending like it didn't hurt to see her turn her attention to other people. But it did. It hurt like hell.

I kept telling myself that maybe it was just the phase we were going through. Maybe she was just distracted. Maybe it had nothing to do with me. But deep down, I knew it wasn't just that. Aarna was pulling away, and I didn't know how to fix it. I didn't know how to tell her what I was feeling—how much I cared about her, how much I needed her in my life.

I kept thinking about what had happened that day at her birthday. When I gave her the keychain with our kindergarten picture. Her eyes. The way she had looked at it. She was touched. I knew it. But something had changed after that. Something in her had shifted, and I couldn't figure out what it was.

Maybe I was being too obvious. Maybe she knew what I was feeling. Maybe she didn't feel the same way, and that was why she was pulling away.

I'd always been so comfortable around Aarna. We didn't need to talk all the time. We didn't need to say anything for it to feel right. But now? Now I felt like I was walking on eggshells, every word, every joke, every little gesture... I was second-guessing everything.

But the thing was—no matter how much she pulled away, no matter how many glances she exchanged with Poorna, it didn't change the fact that Aarna was everything to me. She always had been. She always would be.

I just didn't know how to tell her that without making things worse.

So, I stayed close. I stayed near her, even when she seemed distant. Because deep down, I knew that if I didn't, I might lose her for good. And that was a risk I wasn't willing to take.

9
COINCIDENTS

AARNA

The clock ticked lazily, marking the beginning of my 13th birthday. I couldn't believe it—officially a teenager. Everyone had been telling me how big a deal turning thirteen was. In a way, I was excited. It was my chance to step into a new chapter of my life. But deep inside, I felt a sense of disappointment gnawing at me.

That morning, I had woken up to a simple "Happy Birthday" from my parents. My mom gave me a warm hug, telling me how proud she was of me, and my dad ruffled my hair and teased me about growing up too fast. It was sweet, but still, something felt off. The excitement that should have been there just wasn't.

The day passed in a blur of birthday wishes from friends and family, yet I couldn't shake the feeling that something was missing. It wasn't until the evening, when we went for a quiet dinner at our favorite family restaurant, that things took an unexpected turn.

My parents and I arrived at the restaurant, and I tried to push the thoughts of Rishi away as we walked to our table. The soft chatter and clinking of silverware around us filled the air, but I couldn't stop thinking about how I was never going to be able to forget him. As we settled into our seats, I absentmindedly scanned the room, not expecting to see anything that would catch my attention. But then, I froze.

There, at a table near the far corner, I saw them—Rishi and his family. My heart skipped a beat as I watched him laugh at something his younger brother had said. His eyes were crinkling in that way they always did when he smiled, and my stomach flipped.

I couldn't help it. My eyes lingered on him, hoping—no, longing—for just a moment, a glance. But he was so caught up in his conversation that he didn't notice me. And honestly, a part of me didn't know if I wanted him to.

But then something unexpected happened. As we sat down at our table, Rishi's mom caught sight of us and waved. Rishi turned to look and, for a split second, his eyes met mine.

The surprise on his face was evident. He looked at me, then back at his parents, his cheeks flushing a soft shade of pink. Was he blushing? I couldn't be sure, but something in me stirred. He quickly looked away, clearly flustered, and then his mom waved us over.

"Come, come! Join us! It's Aarna's birthday, right?" she called out, her voice warm and friendly.

My heart leapt in my chest. My parents exchanged glances before agreeing, and we made our way to their table. I felt an odd mix of nerves and excitement as I approached Rishi's family. It was strange, really. Seeing him like this—happy, surrounded by his family—was something I hadn't imagined.

"Happy Birthday, Aarna!" his mom said as we sat down, and his younger brother, Aditya, beamed at me with a big grin. "Hope you're having a great day."

"Thank you!" I smiled, my voice shaky. I noticed that Rishi was staring at his plate now, clearly uncomfortable. But there was still that subtle blush on his cheeks, and I couldn't help but feel a small spark of happiness. He hadn't forgotten.

Rishi looked up at me then, and for a moment, it felt like the world had stopped. His eyes locked with mine, and for the briefest second. Rishi suddenly muttered "Happy Birthday."

"Thank you, Rishi," I whispered, not sure what else to say. He nodded, then quickly looked down again, his face still tinged with pink.

Everyone else continued chatting around us, but I couldn't shake the feeling that this moment was special—something I would remember. Rishi was here, with me, even if it was only for a brief encounter.

"Have you been having a good day?" his mom asked, breaking the silence, and we all turned our attention back to the conversation.

By the time dinner ended, I had to admit, my heart was full in a way I hadn't expected. It wasn't perfect, it wasn't the birthday I had dreamed of, but it was a memory I would treasure. Seeing Rishi again, even just for a few moments, gave me hope that things might one day fall back into place between us.

When we stood to leave, Rishi walked us to the door, his eyes meeting mine one last time before we left the restaurant. He didn't say anything, but I saw the silent apology in his gaze.

And for a moment, I could almost believe that maybe, just maybe, we weren't as far apart as I had thought.

10
THE SEAT

AARNA

A whole year had passed since that awkward birthday. The year I'd spent pretending like I didn't care, burying my emotions under the weight of my schoolwork, and focusing on everything but Rishi. And somehow, here we were—finally in the same class. After all these years of being best friends, of watching him sit a few desks away in different sections, I was now sitting beside him in almost every class. And I still couldn't stop thinking about him.

It was like everything had changed, but nothing had changed at all. When I glanced at him, sitting there, his usual carefree expression, his hand ruffling his hair like it always did when he was thinking—God, I couldn't concentrate.

When I was near him, my heart did this strange little skip, like I'd missed a beat. And I hated it. I had spent so many months telling myself that he was just a friend, that I was just being silly. But the truth was, every time I looked at him, I felt like the world shifted ever so slightly. It felt like... something was there between us. But what? Could he feel it too? Or was it just me, lost in my own confusion?

We were still the same around each other, mostly. I would tease him, like old times, but there was always this... distance. This quiet tension. Something neither of us had addressed, but something that lingered in the air like an unsaid truth. Every time I had to work with him on assignments, it was like my brain short-circuited. I'd forget everything, my hands would get clammy, and I'd stutter over the simplest words. It was embarrassing. How was I supposed to be normal around him when he made everything feel so much more complicated?

Being made class monitors only made it harder. The idea of working with him was both a blessing and a curse. He was always around, always beside me during morning announcements, passing out papers, organizing things—he was never far, which was a good thing, I guess, but it also made my heart race in a way I couldn't control. I was happy, but I was also terrified.

Every time I glanced at him, I wondered if he felt the same way. Or if he'd gotten over it. I couldn't bear the thought of him not caring. And then, when he'd chat casually with Poorna, or laugh with other girls, the jealousy flared up again. The worst part was, I didn't know how to act. Should I be jealous? Should I care? Maybe I shouldn't. Maybe I was overthinking everything.

But the truth was, I couldn't stop thinking about him.

Then, came December 5th, 2017. It started as just another day, with the usual clatter of desks, the shuffle of papers, and the hum of voices filling the room. But when Miss Nisha walked in, holding the new seating arrangement, everything changed.

"Aarna," she said, glancing at the paper. "You'll be sitting next to Rishi for the next month."

And just like that, everything changed.

I tried to act normal—tried to pretend like it wasn't a big deal. I was glad, of course. I mean, we were best friends once. But things had shifted over the last year. I wasn't sure what had changed, or why things had felt so... off. But still, there was this pull. This strange magnetism I couldn't ignore.

Then the reality hit me. He wasn't there. Of course, he wasn't. It was one of those days when he was absent. The timing was perfect, wasn't it?

My heart sank a little. I hadn't expected this. I'd pictured him sitting next to me, joking around like old times, maybe sharing a snack, talking about something random. But instead, there was only an empty chair.

And yet... despite that empty chair, despite the absence of his presence, my mind raced with possibilities. A month of sitting together every day. A whole month. How could I not be excited?

But the excitement was laced with anxiety. How am I supposed to act?

I didn't know what was going on between us anymore. Was I being too obvious? Was he ignoring me on purpose? I couldn't tell. He had his way of staying distant—of making everything seem so casual, so easy. I'd try to talk to him, but sometimes it felt like we were strangers who happened to share the same history. I still teased him, of course. I still pulled his leg like I always did, but I could feel the hesitation now. The distance. It was like he didn't want to be too close, and I didn't know how to bridge that gap.

11
ACROSS THE SILENCE

It was a Thursday morning—just another regular day at school. Or at least, that's what I'd been expecting when I walked into class 7A. I wasn't in the mood for anything special, to be honest. The week had been dragging on, and I was just trying to get through the day. But when I walked into the classroom, I immediately noticed the buzz in the air. Kids were whispering and pointing to the front of the room, where Miss Nisha had just posted the new seating chart on the board.

"Hey, Rishi!" Aarav called from the back of the room, waving me over. "Looks like you've got a new seat!"

I furrowed my brow, confused. "A new seat? What do you mean?"

I pushed through the group of kids crowding around the seating chart and walked up to see what was going on. Miss Nisha, as usual, had been making changes. She glanced up from her desk as I arrived.

"Rishi, you're sitting next to Aarna now," she said, pointing to the spot next to her name.

My heart skipped a beat. Aarna?

I looked over at her. She was sitting quietly at her desk, eyes down, scribbling notes. Just the sight of her sent a rush of memories flooding back.

She was still there. Right next to me.

I hadn't really thought about it until now, but the fact that we were sitting together for the first time in over a year hit me hard. She was the girl I had grown up with—my best friend, the one who had always been by my side. And now... we were strangers. At least, that's how it felt.

"Are you going to just stand there all day?" Aarav teased, nudging me with his elbow.

I snapped out of my thoughts and nodded, making my way to the desk Miss Nisha had pointed out.

Next to Aarna.

It was happening.

I sat down slowly, not knowing exactly how to act. I had no idea what had changed, but everything between us felt... off. It wasn't like the old days when we would talk without a second thought, when sitting next to each other didn't feel so... weird.

I glanced over at her again, but she was still looking down, avoiding eye contact. Was she avoiding me on purpose? Was she just shy? Or was it something else?

I couldn't figure it out.

I had always felt comfortable around Aarna, but now? I didn't know what to say. There was too much history between us, too many unspoken words, and neither of us was brave enough to break the silence.

Miss Nisha started the lesson, and I did my best to focus. But my mind kept drifting back to Aarna. It was impossible not to. There was something about her presence that made everything else feel less important.

We didn't speak all through first period. I kept stealing glances at her, watching her chew on the tip of her pen, the way her hair fell around her face, and how she furrowed her brows when she was focused. She looked the same. But different.

I was nervous. Too nervous.

I felt this strange mix of excitement and fear—like I was on the edge of something, but I didn't know what it was. Part of me wanted to say something, anything, just to fill the awkward silence. But the other part of me was afraid. Afraid of making things worse. Afraid that the distance between us would grow even wider.

I tried to act casual. Focus on the lesson. But it was impossible to ignore the fact that we were sitting together. For the whole day. For the next month.

The bell rang for recess, and I stood up quickly, stretching my legs. I needed a moment to breathe, to shake off the tension that had been building all morning. I could feel the weight of Aarna's presence beside me, and it was both thrilling and terrifying at the same time.

I walked out into the hallway and joined my friends, trying to distract myself. But my thoughts kept drifting back to the classroom. To her.

When I returned, I could see Aarna standing near the door, talking to Nia. She looked at me for a split second—just long enough for our eyes to meet.

My heart skipped a beat.

But she turned away almost immediately.

I stayed by the doorway, pretending to talk to someone, but my eyes kept flicking to her. Why couldn't I just go up to her? Why was it so hard?

By the time we were back in class, I still hadn't said a word to her.

And as the day dragged on, I started to realize something: We were both too shy. Too nervous. Too unsure of what to say.

It was like we were standing on opposite sides of a vast ocean, afraid to take the first step toward each other. Neither of us knew how to break the silence, but we both wanted to.

I just didn't know how.

12

THE SPARK

AARNA

The day had dragged on, and I was starting to feel the pressure of having Rishi sitting next to me. I had spent the morning trying to focus on my work, hoping that the awkwardness would somehow disappear. But it didn't. Every time I looked at him, my heart seemed to skip a beat, and the silence between us stretched longer and longer. I felt like we were strangers. No, we weren't strangers. We had known each other for years—so many years. But sitting next to him felt different now. So different.

I could feel his presence beside me, even when we weren't talking. It was like I was hyper-aware of everything he did—every little movement, every slight sound. The way he tapped his pen on the desk, the way he shuffled his books, the way he occasionally glanced at me, only to look away quickly when our eyes met. Why couldn't he just talk to me?

But then again, why couldn't I talk to him?

I had convinced myself that Rishi liked Poorna. Why else would he be acting so distant? Poorna was the perfect, pretty girl. They always talked in class. They laughed together, and I'd noticed the way he looked at her during lunch breaks. Of course he liked her. It was obvious. And if that was true, then I didn't have a reason to feel this way—this nervousness, this excitement. I should just stop thinking about him.

But I couldn't.

The silence stretched on, and I sat there, tapping my pencil on the desk, trying to focus on the lesson. I needed to stop thinking about Rishi, but it was so hard. Every time I turned my head, I saw him out of the corner of my eye. And every time, my heart raced.

I was trying to finish my notes when I realized that my eraser was missing. I searched my pencil case, but it wasn't there. Frustrated, I glanced over at Rishi. I wasn't sure if he would even respond, but I was running out of options. I had to say something.

"Rishi," I said softly, and then immediately regretted it. My voice had sounded so quiet, almost nervous. What if he didn't hear me? What if he thought I was being weird?

He looked up at me, surprised.

"Yeah?" he asked, his voice a little hesitant.

"I... I don't suppose you have an eraser, do you?" I asked, my words coming out faster than I intended. I felt stupid for asking. It was such a small, insignificant thing, but it felt like a big deal. This was the first time in ages that I'd spoken to him outside of classwork. Was he going to think I was awkward?

There was a long pause. And then, finally, he nodded and reached into his pencil case. He handed me a small, pink eraser.

"Here," he said, his voice softer than usual.

I took it quickly, feeling the heat rush to my cheeks. I couldn't look at him. I was acting like a fool, but I didn't know how to stop it.

I was about to go back to my work when I felt something fall to the floor. My pen. I looked down, and it had rolled under the desk, just out of reach.

"Oh no," I muttered, leaning down to grab it. But before I could, I heard Rishi's voice again.

"I'll get it," he said, and suddenly, we both leaned down at the same time.

Our hands brushed against each other as we both reached for the pen. My breath caught in my throat at the contact. It was just a brief touch, but it felt like an electric shock running through my fingertips.

For a moment, neither of us moved. We just stayed there, kneeling on the floor, our hands close to each other. My pulse was racing. I could feel the warmth from his hand even though we hadn't touched fully. I couldn't look at him. I didn't want to look at him because I was afraid he would see how nervous I was.

I quickly grabbed the pen and straightened up, suddenly feeling very flustered. I could feel my heart thumping in my chest.

"Thanks," I said quickly, my voice barely above a whisper.

Rishi nodded, his face turning slightly pink too. "No problem," he replied.

We sat back down at the same time, the space between us feeling even smaller now, as though the distance that had once existed between us had somehow shrunk. But the silence was still there, hanging heavily in the air. Neither of us knew what to say next.

I wanted to say something. Anything. I wanted to break the tension that had built up over the last year. But I didn't know how.

I glanced at him again, and this time, he was looking at me. For a brief second, our eyes locked. And I felt it again—this strange, inexplicable connection between us. Something I couldn't name, but that I couldn't ignore either.

And then, just as quickly, he looked away, his face turning even more red.

I couldn't help but smile a little. It wasn't a full smile, but it was something. The silence was still there, but it felt different now. Like something had shifted.

Maybe we were getting somewhere. Maybe this was the start of something new.

13

SHARED FEELINGS, UNSPOKEN FEELINGS

RISHI

The class had been going by in a blur. Biology. That meant another hour of Miss Nisha's monotone voice droning on about cells and tissues, but today felt different. The desk next to me—Aarna's desk—felt too close. And yet, too far.

It wasn't like I was complaining. Having Aarna sitting next to me was a dream in some ways. But the silence between us? It was unbearable. Every time I tried to think of something to say, I just... froze. What was wrong with me? She was my friend. But now, sitting so close, she felt more like... something else.

I glanced over at her. She was focused on her textbook, scribbling away in her notes. She looked so studious, the way her brow furrowed slightly when she wrote something down, the way her hair swayed with each movement. It was hard not to be distracted by her, honestly.

But I had a plan today. A stupid one, but one that I hoped would at least get us talking.

I noticed she had her biology textbook open, and I glanced at mine. I had it with me, but I had no intention of using it today. In fact, I had no intention of opening it at all.

So I leaned over to her, trying to act casual. "Aarna," I whispered, tapping my pen on my notebook, "I didn't bring my biology textbook today." I knew it was a lie. I had my textbook tucked right under my arm, but I was hoping she'd fall for it. I had to find a way to share hers with her. To be near her.

She glanced up at me, her eyes narrowing slightly, a slight frown on her face. "Really, Rishi? You forgot your book?" she asked, raising an eyebrow. She didn't look convinced.

I shrugged, trying to look as casual as possible. "Yeah, guess I didn't pack it today."

For a moment, she just stared at me. Her gaze softened, and then she sighed, pulling her textbook closer to her. "Fine. You can share mine," she muttered, pushing the book towards me.

My heart skipped a beat. I didn't expect it to be that easy. I felt a grin tugging at the corners of my mouth, but I tried to hide it. I didn't want her to know how happy I was to be sitting next to her, sharing a book. But it was the perfect excuse to stay close, to not have to deal with the awkward silence. I was this close to breaking it.

Before I could say anything, Sakshi, Aarna's best friend, leaned forward from the next row, overhearing the conversation. Of course, she did. She was always so observant, and right now, I could practically see the mischief lighting up in her eyes.

"Rishi, seriously?" she teased, leaning in with that same smirk she always wore when she caught me in a lie. "You don't have your book? What are you gonna do, sit next to Aarna and share her book all day?"

My stomach dropped. I wasn't sure whether I was embarrassed or relieved that she was calling me out so openly.

Aarna glanced at me, then back at Sakshi, her lips curling into a small, teasing smile. "You're one to talk, Sakshi. I think Rishi's just being polite," she said, not missing a beat.

Sakshi raised an eyebrow, clearly not buying it. "Oh, I see," she said with a knowing grin, "You two are definitely gonna share more than just books, huh?"

I could feel my face heating up. Sakshi wasn't even trying to hide the teasing anymore. Aarna didn't seem bothered by it, though. She just rolled her eyes and muttered something under her breath about "being so dramatic," but I knew she was secretly enjoying the attention.

Sakshi looked satisfied, sitting back in her seat, clearly happy to have poked fun at me. Aarna, meanwhile, just turned to me, opening her textbook wide for me to see the page we were on. She didn't even say anything, just slid the book toward me and focused back on her notes.

I leaned closer, trying to pay attention, but it was hard. The pages blurred together, and my mind kept wandering. I couldn't stop noticing the way her fingers brushed against the page as she flipped it, the way her head tilted slightly when she tried to concentrate, the faint smell of her perfume... How could I focus on biology when she was sitting right here next to me?

I felt like I had a thousand things to say, but nothing came out. Every time I looked over at her, I could feel my heart race. And she—she—seemed completely unaware of the effect she had on me.

But soon enough, it became clear that neither of us was actually paying attention to the lesson. We were sharing the book, but neither of us was really reading it. Every time I tried to focus, I found myself getting distracted by Aarna's soft voice when she whispered a question about something in the chapter or by the way her pen tapped against the page in thought.

By the end of the period, we hadn't taken any notes. And the worst part? I realized neither of us had even looked at the textbook for more than a few seconds at a time.

Later that week, Miss Nisha handed out the biology test results, and I could see the frustration on Aarna's face as she scanned the paper. She hadn't done well. Not by a long shot.

I didn't know what to say. I felt guilty. It was my fault. I had been so distracted by being close to her, by just sharing a textbook with her, that I hadn't noticed how much we had both missed in class.

And now, here she was—looking disappointed, trying to hide the fact that she had failed the test.

I wanted to apologize, to tell her it was my fault, but instead, I just stayed silent, watching her from across the room as she tucked her paper into her bag. The silence between us felt different now. Heavier. And I hated it.

I just wished I could go back to that moment, sit beside her without all the awkwardness, without all the stupid distractions. But I knew it was too late now.

All I could do was hope that next time—whenever that was—she wouldn't be sitting next to me again, distracted by me.

14

CONFESSION

AARNA

Things had finally started to feel normal again. The silence between Rishi and me had softened, and even though it was still awkward at times, we were back on track. We weren't exactly the best of friends yet, but we weren't strangers either. And honestly, I was okay with that. It was... better than nothing.

But more importantly, I didn't have to worry about biology anymore, thanks to Rishi.

The past few weeks, he had been helping me a lot, especially in subjects where I wasn't so confident—chemistry and physics. He'd noticed that I struggled in those classes, and though I'd been too proud to ask for help at first, I was glad he'd stepped in.

He was patient with me, and whenever I asked questions, he never made me feel dumb. He'd explain concepts again and again if I didn't get them the first time, sometimes in ways that even made sense to me (which is saying a lot, since chemistry was still a foreign language to me).

I tried not to let him see how much I appreciated it, but there were moments when I was sure he could tell. I mean, it's hard not to notice when someone looks at you with that... look of admiration in their eyes, right?

I didn't have to tell him he was helping me so much—he could just tell. It felt nice, though. Nice to know that we were finally talking again, even if it wasn't about us. Even if it wasn't about what I really wanted to know.

And what I wanted to know, more than anything, was what was going on in his mind.

I had been thinking about it for days now.

Did Rishi like me?

I'd been circling around that question for weeks, but I still couldn't get a clear answer. Every time I looked at him, I felt that flutter in my stomach. I'd caught him glancing at me too—whether it was when we were sharing notes in class or during lunch, there was always that moment when our eyes met, and I'd see something—something—there. But what was it? Was it friendship? Or was it something else?

I had to know.

And I wasn't going to sit around waiting for him to tell me. I had a plan.

I'd been thinking about it all week, brainstorming with Sakshi. I had to know what Rishi was feeling, and the only way to find out was by asking. Or, better yet, getting him to tell me without directly asking.

Sakshi had been surprisingly supportive of this, even if she was a bit too enthusiastic about the whole thing. She told me to "go for it" and that she'd help me with whatever I needed.

I was determined to figure it out once and for all. So on 12th December 2017, I decided to take matters into my own hands.

I settled into my seat next to him, trying to act normal, even though my heart was beating so fast I thought it might burst out of my chest. He didn't say anything right away, but I could feel him glancing at me every now and then, his eyes soft but unreadable.

I wasn't going to wait for him to speak first.

I turned slightly towards him, trying to sound casual. "Hey, Rishi," I started, my voice steady even though my insides were twisting with nervous energy, "I was thinking... do you have like a crush on anybody?."

Rishi raised an eyebrow, clearly surprised. "What?"

"Let's pass chits," I said quickly, my words tumbling out before I could second-guess myself. "We write down the name of the person we have a crush on and exchange them."

He stared at me for a moment, clearly unsure about the whole idea. "You want to do that... now?"

I nodded. "Yeah, why not? It's harmless. And, you know, fun."

There was a long pause. I could see him thinking, his brow furrowing slightly. But then, after a beat, he shrugged. "Alright, fine. If you say so."

I reached into my bag and tore a piece of paper out of my notebook. I quickly folded it into a small square, then handed it to him. I could feel my hands trembling just slightly as I passed it to him. Rishi took the paper without saying anything, his fingers brushing against mine for a split second.

My breath caught in my throat.

I tried not to make it obvious, but I was struggling to keep calm. I didn't know what he was going to write, and part of me was scared—what if he wrote someone else's name? What if he didn't like me at all? But then again, what if he did? So because of this confusion, i decided to leave the chit blank.

I watched as he scribbled something down, his pen moving quickly across the paper. He folded it, not looking up at me, and handed it back.

Without a word, I took the chit from him, my heart pounding in my chest. This was it. The moment I'd been waiting for.

I opened the chit slowly, feeling my hands shake. The paper felt so fragile in my grip, like it was the key to everything I needed to know.

I looked down at the paper. And then I froze.

He just looked at me, his gaze intense but unreadable. And then, without another word, he reached over to me and slid his chit toward me, the folded paper silently crossing the desk between us.

And there, in neat handwriting, was a name.

Aarna.

I froze. My heart skipped a beat.

He wrote my name.

My chest tightened, my breath catching in my throat. I couldn't speak, couldn't even think clearly for a moment. I just stared at the paper in my hands, trying to process what had just happened.

I glanced over at Rishi, but he was looking away, his gaze fixed on the front of the class, as if he was pretending like nothing had changed.

But everything had changed.

My mind raced, and I could feel a blush creeping up my neck.

Rishi had written my name.

I wanted to say something, but I couldn't find the words. What was there to say? He had already told me, in the simplest, most honest way he knew how.

I cleared my throat, trying to steady my voice. "Rishi," I whispered, and when he looked at me, I felt my heart drop. "You... you like me?"

Rishi nodded, his expression softening. "I think I've always liked you," he said quietly, his voice barely above a whisper.

15
CHITPASSING

RISHI

I couldn't stop thinking about it. The chit. The blank one Aarna had given me.

Every time I closed my eyes, I saw it again. Empty. No name. No clue.

I had hoped—no, I had believed—that today was the day I'd finally find out how she felt about me. But that blank chit... it hit me harder than I expected. I wasn't angry, but I couldn't shake the feeling of disappointment.

Why didn't she write anything? Did she not like me at all? Was I imagining things?

I'd been helping her with chemistry and physics, sitting next to her, and for the first time in what felt like forever, we were back to being comfortable around each other. But that one moment—the chit—had thrown everything into question.

I couldn't concentrate in class. I was restless. Fidgeting with my pen, tapping my foot under the desk. Every time I tried to focus on what Miss Nisha was saying, my mind wandered back to the moment I opened the chit. The blank space.

What did it mean? Was she playing games with me? Or was I just overthinking everything?

"Rishi," Miss Nisha's voice broke through my thoughts, sharp and clear. "Hand in your paper."

I snapped out of my thoughts, my hands almost shaking as I picked up my biology assignment. My heart was still pounding in my chest, and I felt a weird mix of frustration and nervousness.

I handed her my paper and quickly sat back down. But something in my gut told me that I wasn't going to get any answers today.

That's when I saw Aarna. She was staring at me, her expression a little distant, like she was lost in her own thoughts too. Then, as if she hadn't already driven me crazy enough, I saw her take out a piece of paper.

My heart skipped a beat. Was she going to write something? Was she going to do what I had hoped she would do earlier—tell me how she felt?

I watched her, barely breathing, as she scribbled something on the paper. But before I could even make sense of it, she folded the chit and slid it across the desk toward me.

I froze.

My pulse quickened, but this time it wasn't out of excitement—it was pure anxiety. She had written something.

I grabbed the chit quickly, my hands slightly trembling, and opened it, only to find two simple letters: "YOU."

I stared at the words, my eyes wide in disbelief.

You?

My heart soared. It was like a wave of relief and joy hit me all at once, flooding my chest with warmth. It was the simplest thing, but the fact that she had written "YOU" told me everything I needed to know.

She likes me. She really likes me.

I couldn't contain myself.

I stood up so suddenly that my chair almost tipped over, ignoring the confused looks from my classmates. I wasn't thinking anymore, I wasn't caring about anything else. All I could feel was the rush of excitement, and without even thinking, I bolted out of the classroom.

I ran straight for the washroom.

I pushed the door open and, without any hesitation, I started dancing.

I danced like a madman, completely losing myself in the moment.

I spun around, laughing out loud. I didn't care that I was alone or that people would probably think I was crazy. All that mattered was that Aarna had written you. She liked me.

I couldn't stop smiling.

Just as I was spinning around in an overly dramatic fashion, I heard the door creak open.

I stopped mid-spin, half-expecting to be caught in the act of my embarrassing little dance routine. But it was just Harsh, looking slightly confused but amused.

He leaned against the doorframe, raising an eyebrow. "What are you doing?"

I grinned like an idiot. "I'm dancing. I just got a sign. A good sign."

Harsh smirked. "Oh, really? Let me guess—Aarna gave you a chit with her name on it?"

I froze. How did he know? Had he seen it?

"Uhh..." I scratched the back of my head, suddenly self-conscious. "Sort of. She wrote 'YOU'." I couldn't help but smile again, like I was the happiest person alive.

Harsh chuckled. "Man, I don't think I've ever seen you this happy. I can tell you're crazy about her."

I nodded vigorously, still beaming. "You don't even know. I thought I was going crazy. But now I know."

"You two are something else," Harsh said, shaking his head, a small smile on his face. "But seriously, Rishi, she's definitely into you. That chit? She wouldn't have written that if she wasn't. Trust me."

I let out a laugh, still processing everything. "I know, I know. I just—" I stopped myself, not knowing how to explain the feeling. "It's just... everything feels so right now. I don't even know how to handle it."

Harsh grinned, then turned to leave the washroom, but not before he gave me one last piece of advice. "Look, man, you've got to tell her. The whole 'acting clueless' thing? It's cute, but if you don't make a move soon, she's going to think you're not interested."

I blinked at him, realizing he was probably right. I had to say something to Aarna. I couldn't keep dancing around the truth anymore.

I returned to class with a huge grin on my face, and I'm pretty sure I was still humming from the little dance party I'd had with myself in the washroom. I walked in just as Miss Nisha was handing back papers.

I caught Aarna's eye and couldn't help but smile even wider. She smiled back shyly, and for a moment, it felt like we were the only two people in the room.

16
SECRETS IN THE NIGHT

AARNA

Since the confession, life had felt like walking on clouds—soft, surreal, and a little dangerous. Rishi and I talked every night, huddled in the shadows of secrecy. The landline in my room had become our lifeline, a bridge between two houses where prying eyes and ears could never intrude.

Tonight was no different. I tiptoed into my room after dinner, my heart beating faster with every step. Mom's words echoed in my head: "Stay focused on your studies, Aarna. You don't want distractions ruining your future."

If only she knew.

I locked the door softly, careful not to make a sound. The bulky beige receiver sat on my desk, waiting. With trembling fingers, I dialed his number, memorized after so many nights of practice. It rang once. Twice.

"Hello?" Rishi's voice was a whisper, yet it held the warmth of a thousand sunrises.

"It's me," I said, my voice hushed but filled with relief.

"Finally," he breathed. "I thought you'd never call. Did your mom give you one of her lecture marathons?"

I chuckled, leaning back in my chair. "No, but she was hovering around the kitchen for ages. What about your parents?"

"Busy watching some soap opera. I slipped out during the dramatic wedding scene," he teased.

The sound of his laughter always made me smile. "We should be studying, you know," I said, though my heart wasn't in the reprimand.

"We will," he promised. "But tell me first—how was your day?"

And just like that, the conversation flowed. We shared everything, from mundane moments to whispered dreams. Rishi talked about how his friends teased him endlessly, claiming they knew about us. I told him about the time I accidentally blushed when someone mentioned his name.

"You blushed?" he asked, his tone laced with amusement.

"I hate you," I said, though the grin on my face said otherwise.

"Admit it, Aarna. You like me a little too much."

I rolled my eyes, even though he couldn't see me. "Shut up, Rishi."

But beneath the playful banter, there was always an edge of caution. Every rustle outside my room made my heart skip a beat. Every muffled sound from his end made me fear someone had picked up the extension.

"What if they find out?" I asked suddenly, the thought clawing at the edges of my mind.

"They won't," he said firmly. "We're careful."

"But for how long?" My voice wavered, betraying the worry I had tried to bury.

"For as long as it takes," he replied. "Aarna, we'll get through this. We just need to be patient. And focused."

That word—focused—had become our mantra. Despite the fluttering hearts and stolen moments, we both knew what was at stake. Our parents had dreams for us, expectations as heavy as the textbooks stacked on our desks. And we had promised each other that no matter what, we wouldn't let this love derail those dreams.

"Alright," I said, straightening in my chair. "Let's study. What's your plan for math?"

Rishi groaned theatrically. "Math? Really? I thought we were escaping reality here."

"Rishi," I said, my voice a mock warning.

"Fine, fine. But don't expect miracles," he muttered.

We spent the next hour quizzing each other, laughing at our mistakes, and debating over the correct approach to trigonometric problems. Somewhere in between, the line between love and friendship blurred, creating a bond that felt unshakable.

But even in the comfort of his voice, the shadows of our reality lingered. The secrecy, the lies, the constant fear of being caught—it was exhausting. Yet, I couldn't imagine a life without these moments, without him.

"Okay, enough math," Rishi said finally. "Tell me something. If we could go anywhere right now, where would it be?"

"Anywhere?" I asked, closing my eyes.

"Anywhere," he said softly.

I thought for a moment, letting my mind wander. "The beach. Somewhere quiet, with no one around. Just us, listening to the waves."

He was silent for a moment, and I wondered if he was imagining it too. "That sounds perfect," he said. "One day, Aarna. I promise."

A noise outside my room snapped me back to reality. Mom's footsteps were unmistakable, growing louder with each passing second.

"I have to go," I whispered hurriedly.

"Alright. Sweet dreams, Aarna," he said, his voice tender.

"You too, Rishi."

I hung up just as Mom knocked on my door. "Aarna, are you asleep?"

"No, Mom," I called back, flipping open my textbook. "Just studying."

"Good. Don't stay up too late."

"I won't."

The sound of her retreating footsteps eased the tension in my chest. But as I stared at the pages of my book, the words blurred into a mess of ink. My mind was still with Rishi, his voice echoing in my thoughts.

This love, as tangled and fragile as it was, gave me strength. And as I turned off the light and climbed into bed, I clung to the promise we had made—to hold on, to focus, and to find our way together.

17
LOVE ON THE BOARD

RISHI

I walked into school that morning with a stupid grin on my face. The memory of last night's conversation with Aarna played on a loop in my head, her laughter still ringing in my ears.

Of course, my friends were quick to ruin the peaceful morning.

"Look who's glowing today!" Arjun smirked as he leaned against my desk. "Late-night calls, huh?"

"Shut up," I muttered, trying to focus on unpacking my bag. But that only fueled their excitement.

"Oh, come on, Rishi," Anuj chimed in, dropping his bag onto the chair beside mine. "We all know what's going on. 'Just friends' my foot!"

The rest of the group erupted into laughter, and I sighed, knowing there was no point in denying it. My cheeks betrayed me anyway, flushing a shade of red that they wouldn't let me live down.

"What did you two talk about? Plans for the weekend? Love letters disguised as math notes?" Arjun teased.

"Focus on your studies for once," I shot back, hoping to divert their attention.

Anuj snorted. "Oh, we're focused alright. Focused on how whipped you are."

I rolled my eyes, but a small smile tugged at the corners of my lips. Teasing or not, it was impossible to be mad at them.

The bell rang, signaling the start of the day, and the teasing subsided—at least for a while. But during recess, the mischief started again.

While I was busy eating lunch, Anuj decided to be his usual annoying self. "Rishi, don't be mad, but I did something hilarious," he said, his tone suggesting that I should definitely be mad.

"What did you do now?" I asked warily.

"Oh, nothing major," he said with a grin. "Just a little masterpiece on the whiteboard."

The way he said it made my stomach drop. "What kind of masterpiece?"

"You'll see," he said, looking way too pleased with himself.

I didn't have time to press him further because the bell rang again, and we all hurried back to class. As I walked in, I froze.

There it was, in big, bold letters on the whiteboard:
Aarna ♥ Rishi

My stomach sank. "Anuj," I hissed, glaring at him.

"What? It's true, isn't it?" he said with a smug grin, clearly proud of his handiwork.

"Erase it!" I said, my voice low and urgent.

"Relax, she'll love it," he said, shrugging as he took his seat.

I grabbed the duster, but it was too late. Just as I reached the board, Aarna walked in.

Her eyes went straight to the words. She froze, her expression shifting from surprise to anger in a matter of seconds.

"Aarna, wait—" I started, but she cut me off with a sharp glare.

"Who did this?" she demanded, her voice cold.

Anuj raised his hand, looking unbothered. "That would be me. Impressive, right?"

"You think this is funny?" she snapped, marching up to him.

Anuj leaned back in his chair, looking unfazed. "Come on, Aarna. It's just a joke. Lighten up."

"A joke?" she repeated, her voice rising. "You think it's funny to embarrass me in front of the entire class? To put my name up there without my permission?"

The room fell silent. Even the students who usually loved a bit of drama stopped what they were doing to watch.

Anuj's smug grin faltered. "I didn't mean anything by it. It's not a big deal."

"Not a big deal?" Aarna's eyes flashed. "Do you have any idea how humiliating this is? I don't need you playing cupid with my life!"

She grabbed the duster from my hand and erased the board in one swift motion. The sound of the duster hitting the surface was sharp, almost as sharp as her words.

"Next time you think about pulling a stunt like this, don't," she said, her tone icy. "Because it's not your business."

Anuj mumbled something under his breath, but Aarna didn't stick around to listen. She stalked back to her seat, her face a mixture of anger and hurt.

I wanted to say something, to explain that I hadn't been a part of this, but the look she gave me as I opened my mouth was enough to silence me.

The rest of the day was a blur. No matter how many times I tried to talk to her, she ignored me. She wouldn't even glance in my direction.

By the time the final bell rang, I felt like I had aged a decade. As we packed up, I tried one last time. "Aarna, can we talk?"

She didn't even pause. "I have nothing to say," she said, her tone clipped, before walking out of the room.

I stood there, feeling a mix of frustration and guilt. Anuj's stupid joke had gone too far, and now I had to fix it. But how?

As I walked home that evening, I replayed the moment over and over in my head, trying to figure out what to say to her. Aarna was never one to hold grudges, but something about this felt different.

I didn't know how, but I would make it right. I had to.

18
A LINE BETWEEN US

AARNA

The soft chime of the landline rang out for the third time that evening. I didn't need to guess who it was—I already knew.

Rishi.

I stared at the receiver from where I sat, curled up on the sofa with my history textbook. My heart wanted to answer, but my anger held me back. The memory of the whiteboard still stung, the laughter of my classmates echoing in my mind.

The phone rang again, persistent. My fingers twitched, hovering over the edge of my textbook.

"Mumma, I'll get it!" I called out before she could ask about the relentless ringing.

But instead of answering, I let it ring out. And then it stopped.

For a moment, the silence felt satisfying, but it was quickly replaced by guilt. I knew he'd keep calling.

The phone started again. I closed my eyes and sighed.

This time, I grabbed it. Not to answer, but to hang up quickly before it disturbed the entire house. My heart thudded as I held it in my hand, staring at the familiar digits on the caller ID.

I hung up.

Minutes passed, the guilt gnawing at me. I tried to focus on my textbook, reading the same line over and over again until it blurred together. But I couldn't. Not when I knew he was trying so hard to reach me.

Finally, I caved. The anger had started to lose its edge, leaving room for something else: curiosity, maybe even understanding. I dialed his number, my fingers moving on their own.

It rang twice before he picked up.

"Aarna!" His voice was a mix of relief and panic.

I didn't say anything at first. Let him sweat a little, I thought, even though the sound of his voice softened me.

"Aarna, please listen to me. I swear, I didn't have anything to do with what Anuj did. You know how he is, always trying to get a laugh out of everything."

"You didn't stop him either," I said, my tone sharper than I intended.

"I didn't know he'd do something so stupid! I was eating lunch when he wrote that. I tried to erase it, but you walked in before I could."

I stayed silent, my mind flashing back to the look on his face when I entered the classroom. He had looked panicked, not smug like Anuj.

"I promise, Aarna, I'd never embarrass you like that. You believe me, don't you?"

There was something earnest in his voice that made it hard to stay angry. I sighed, leaning back against the couch.

"I don't know, Rishi," I admitted. "It's just... I don't like being the center of attention like that. It's embarrassing."

"I know. And I'm sorry you had to go through that. I told Anuj he went too far."

I traced invisible patterns on the cushion beside me, thinking.

"Maybe," I began hesitantly, "maybe we shouldn't make it so obvious to everyone. About... us."

There was a pause on the other end of the line, and for a moment, I worried he'd be upset.

"You mean, keep things low-key?" he asked.

"Yeah. It's not like I want to hide it," I clarified quickly, "but maybe we don't give them anything to tease us about. At least for now."

He was quiet for a moment before he said, "If that's what you want, then okay. I get it. And, Aarna..."

"Yes?"

"I really am sorry. For everything."

I smiled despite myself, the last traces of my anger melting away. "Okay. I believe you."

"Does that mean you're not mad at me anymore?" he asked, his voice lighter now, almost playful.

"Not at you," I said. "But if Anuj tries something like that again..."

"I'll handle him," Rishi promised. "You won't have to worry about it."

"Good," I said, feeling a small sense of satisfaction.

For the first time that day, I felt lighter. The weight of the incident at school didn't seem as heavy anymore.

"Get some sleep, Rishi," I said softly.

"You too," he replied.

I hung up the phone, a small smile lingering on my lips. Maybe we didn't have it all figured out, but at least we were trying.

19
COLORS OF HOPE

RISHI

Exams have this way of making life feel monotonous. Aarna and I hadn't spoken much since that evening, and I wasn't sure if it was because we were both buried in our books or because something still lingered unspoken between us.

But even with the weight of exam stress pressing down on me, there was one thing keeping me motivated: the Kaleidoscope Art Event at St. William's College.

Art has always been my escape. My room is my sanctuary, its walls covered with my paintings, sketches stacked on every surface. I pour every bit of myself into those canvases—the chaos, the calm, everything in between.

The thought of the event sent a spark of excitement through me. Just the idea of being surrounded by people who shared the same passion, of seeing their creativity come to life, felt like a dream. And this wasn't just any event—it was the event, the one everyone talked about.

I glanced at the flyer pinned to the corner of my corkboard, the bold letters announcing: "Kaleidoscope: A Celebration of Art and Imagination."

"I have to get selected," I muttered to myself, flipping through my sketchbook for ideas.

The selection process was simple but nerve-wracking: submit three pieces that best represent your style. My style. How do you even define that? My work was all over the place—abstract splashes of color, realistic portraits, even a few pencil sketches of random moments I'd tried to capture.

I stopped at one sketch: Aarna, sitting on a bench in the schoolyard, her hair falling over her face as she scribbled furiously in her notebook. I'd drawn it months ago, back when things between us were simple, easy.

For a moment, I wondered if I should include it. But then I shook my head. This wasn't about her—it was about me.

I flipped to another page, my mind already racing through ideas.

Later that evening, I sat cross-legged on the floor of my room, surrounded by a mess of supplies: brushes, tubes of paint, scraps of paper. My favorite canvas leaned against the wall, half-finished.

The scene was vivid in my mind—a burst of colors swirling together, chaotic yet harmonious. It wasn't something I could explain with words, but I knew what it felt like.

I dipped my brush into a deep blue, then swirled it onto the canvas. The color spread like a ripple, blending into the fiery orange streaks I'd painted earlier.

As I worked, time seemed to blur. Hours passed, but I didn't care. This was my world, my rhythm. The stress of exams, the awkward silence with Aarna, everything faded into the background.

By the time I stepped back to look at my work, it was nearly midnight. My shoulders ached, and there were streaks of paint on my hands, but I felt a sense of accomplishment.

It wasn't perfect—not yet. But it was mine.

I turned to the other two pieces I'd decided to submit: a pencil sketch of an old man sitting by the river, his expression serene yet heavy with untold stories, and an abstract piece of intertwined lines and shapes, inspired by the chaos of city life.

All three pieces felt like fragments of me, snapshots of how I saw the world.

The next day at school, I packed the artwork carefully into a portfolio and handed it to the art teacher for submission.

"Good luck, Rishi," she said with a smile.

"Thanks, ma'am," I replied, trying to hide how nervous I felt.

For the rest of the day, my mind was split between the exams and the event. Aarna walked past me in the hallway once, her focus fixed on a notebook in her hand. I wanted to call out to her, but something held me back.

I told myself it was better this way. We both had things to focus on, and right now, I needed to give this art submission my all.

That night, as I lay in bed, my mind raced with thoughts of the event. What if I wasn't good enough? What if I didn't make it?

But then I thought about the colors on the canvas, the way they came alive under my hands. This was my passion, my escape. Even if I didn't get selected, at least I knew I'd poured my heart into it.

And maybe, just maybe, Aarna would notice.

20

UNFOLDING COLORS

AARNA

The art room smelled like fresh paint and old memories. I stood in front of the large bulletin board, staring at the announcement about the Kaleidoscope Art Event.

I had walked past this board a dozen times in the past week, hesitating every single time. Submitting my work felt... personal, like putting a piece of my soul on display. But today, something was different. Maybe it was the way the light filtered through the windows, illuminating the board like a spotlight, or maybe it was the little voice in my head telling me, Why not?

My sketchbook felt heavy in my hands as I flipped through the pages, searching for the right pieces. There was a watercolor painting of a solitary tree on a hill, its branches reaching out like arms craving the sky. Then there was the charcoal sketch of a dancer mid-spin, her movements frozen in time. Finally, there was the piece that made my heart flutter every time I looked at it—a pastel drawing of a sunrise over the ocean, inspired by a family trip years ago.

I wasn't sure if they were good enough, but something inside me whispered, Just try.

The art teacher looked up from her desk as I approached.

"Miss Patel, submitting for Kaleidoscope?" she asked with a smile.

"Yes, ma'am," I replied, handing over my sketchbook with slightly trembling hands.

She flipped through the pages, nodding approvingly. "These are lovely, Aarna. You've got a good eye."

"Thank you, ma'am."

As I walked out of the art room, I felt lighter, as though a weight I hadn't realized I was carrying had been lifted. I hadn't told anyone about my submission—not even Rishi. It wasn't intentional; I just wanted to do this for myself.

The next day at school, the buzz about the event was louder than ever. During lunch, I overheard snippets of conversations about submissions and expectations. I sat with my friends, pretending to focus on my food, but my ears perked up when someone mentioned Rishi.

"Did you hear?" Anuj said, loud enough for the whole cafeteria to hear. "Rishi submitted his artwork for Kaleidoscope!"

My fork froze mid-air.

I turned to him, trying to keep my expression neutral. "Rishi submitted?"

"Yeah," Anuj said with a grin. "The guy's room is practically an art gallery. No surprise there."

A strange mix of emotions swirled inside me. Pride? Excitement? Nerves? I hadn't expected him to submit, and now, the thought of both of us being in the running felt... surreal.

Later that day, I bumped into Rishi in the hallway.

"Hey," I said, trying to sound casual.

"Hey," he replied, his usual smile tugging at his lips. "What's up?"

"I heard you submitted for Kaleidoscope," I said, watching his reaction carefully.

His smile faltered for a fraction of a second. "Yeah, I did. Why?"

I hesitated. "Because I did too."

The look on his face was priceless. His eyes widened in surprise, and then a slow smile spread across his face.

"Wait—you submitted?" he asked, sounding almost incredulous.

I nodded, feeling a little self-conscious under his gaze. "Why is that so surprising?"

"It's not," he said quickly. "I just... I didn't know."

"Well, now you do."

When the day of the results arrived, the entire school seemed to gather around the bulletin board. My heart raced as I pushed through the crowd, trying to catch a glimpse of the list.

"Raj, Soham, Rishi..." someone read aloud.

"And Aarna!" another voice added.

My breath caught. I made it.

"Rishi, you made it!" I turned to him instinctively, my excitement bubbling over.

He grinned at me, his eyes shining with pride. "So did you!"

In that moment, the awkwardness of the past few days melted away. Standing there, surrounded by the chatter of our classmates, I felt like everything was falling into place.

Kaleidoscope wasn't just about art anymore—it was about us, about this strange, tangled journey we were on together.

21

KALEIDOSCOPE

AARNA

The venue for the Kaleidoscope Art Event was nothing short of breathtaking. St. William's College had transformed its auditorium into a colorful haven, with white walls covered in vibrant, thought-provoking art. The buzz of excitement filled the air as participants set up their pieces, preparing to showcase their work to the crowd.

The theme for the event was "Something You're Grateful For."

I glanced around at the other participants, each of them already immersed in their art, carefully positioning their canvases. I wasn't sure if I was nervous or just thrilled to be here. My mind kept wandering back to the piece I had created—a bold, abstract design of overlapping shapes and colors. It represented the unexpected moments of life that make everything feel whole. The piece wasn't a portrait or a literal representation of gratitude, but it felt right. It was everything that I couldn't put into words.

As I set my artwork on its stand, I felt a hand on my shoulder. I turned to see Rishi, holding his canvas with a smile.

"Hey," he said, his voice a little shaky, but his eyes brimming with excitement.

"Hey," I replied, giving him a reassuring smile. "You ready?"

He glanced at the crowd gathering, then at his own artwork—my portrait, captured beautifully in soft pencil strokes with delicate shading. There was something so intimate about it, so personal. He had drawn me as if I was the very thing he was grateful for.

"It's just a sketch," Rishi said, brushing it off, though the pride in his eyes said otherwise.

"It's beautiful," I told him.

"Thanks." He smiled, stepping back.

I couldn't help but notice the way he looked at me, as if my presence in his life was the most natural thing in the world. And in that moment, I realized I felt the same.

The event kicked off, and one by one, participants were called to present their work. I stood next to my piece, watching as people admired the abstract shapes and bright colors that represented life's many facets.

When Rishi's turn came, he stood up with quiet confidence, explaining his piece—the portrait of me—and how he was grateful for the little moments of stillness we shared in our busy lives. I felt my heart flutter, but I forced myself to look away.

The judges made their rounds, offering compliments and insights. The tension in the air was palpable as we waited for the results to be announced.

Finally, the host stepped up to the microphone.

"Let's announce the winners!" she said, and the room went silent.

She smiled as she read from the list.

"First place, the winner of the Kaleidoscope Art Event is... Rishi!"

I couldn't help but clap loudly as Rishi stood, a surprised grin spreading across his face. He was speechless, his hands shaking as he accepted the award.

But the moment didn't last long. Raj, Rishi's best friend, leaned in from behind and said loudly, "Congrats, bro! Now I'm going to have to call Aarna my sister-in-law!"

The whole room erupted into laughter. Rishi turned red, but his laughter was contagious as he shot a playful glare at Raj.

"Well, you know, she's basically family now."

Raj, not one to be left out of the limelight, was quickly called up to accept the consolation prize. He made a grand show of it, bowing dramatically to the audience, much to the amusement of everyone around.

Then the host turned to the final award.

"And the 'Best Ideation' award goes to… Aarna!"

I blinked in shock. My heart skipped as I walked to the front to accept the plaque. I hadn't expected this. Not at all. But as I looked at Rishi from across the room, I saw that familiar, encouraging smile. He was proud of me.

Later, after the ceremony, as the crowd began to thin out, Rishi and I found ourselves alone near the back of the venue.

"So… you really think I'm grateful for you?" Rishi teased, glancing at his award.

I grinned, trying to fight the butterflies in my stomach. "I don't know… you did draw me."

He shrugged, a mischievous glint in his eye. "It's not the worst thing I could have done."

I laughed softly. "Thanks, Rishi. For everything."

He stepped closer, his voice suddenly quieter. "No, thank you, Aarna. You make everything feel… easier."

Our eyes met, and for a moment, the rest of the world melted away. The noise of the event, the awkwardness of our past few days, everything seemed to vanish. It was just the two of us, standing there, connected by something unspoken but deeply felt.

And in that quiet, shared moment, I realized that the colors of gratitude weren't just on our canvases—they were in the space between us, where everything else faded into the background.

The Kaleidoscope Art Event had officially come to an end, and the chatter of participants and spectators began to fade as people made their way home. Rishi and I lingered a little longer than necessary, the glow of the evening still fresh in our minds.

As we stepped out of the venue, the night greeted us with a cool breeze. The city lights twinkled like a million tiny stars, and the distant hum of traffic made everything feel alive.

"I guess we should head home," I said, clutching the plaque I'd won.

"Yeah," Rishi replied, his hands shoved into his pockets.

We both glanced up and down the street, searching for a cab, but the roads seemed unusually empty for a Saturday night.

"No cabs," Rishi said, stating the obvious.

I sighed. "Looks like we're walking."

"Not the worst thing," he said with a smirk.

And so, we started walking.

The road stretched ahead of us, lined with dimly lit streetlights and the occasional honk of a passing car. It wasn't a long walk, maybe twenty minutes at most, but something about it felt… different.

The breeze tousled my hair, and I found myself hugging my arms as the chill set in.

"Cold?" Rishi asked, glancing over at me.

"A little," I admitted.

Without a word, he slipped off his jacket and draped it over my shoulders.

"Rishi, you don't have to—"

"Just take it," he said, his tone leaving no room for argument.

I pulled the jacket tighter around me, the warmth and faint scent of him making me smile.

"You're annoyingly nice sometimes, you know that?" I said, half-joking.

He chuckled. "I'll take that as a compliment."

We walked in comfortable silence for a while, the rhythm of our steps syncing as we moved through the quiet streets. The event still lingered in my mind, but more than that, I kept replaying little moments from the day—Rishi's drawing, his grin when he won, the way he looked at me during the ceremony.

"You know," I began, breaking the silence, "today turned out pretty amazing."

Rishi glanced at me, a soft smile playing on his lips. "Yeah, it did."

"I'm still surprised you won," I teased, nudging him lightly.

"Hey!" he protested, feigning offense. "I worked hard on that sketch."

"I'm kidding," I said, laughing. "It was beautiful. You deserved it."

His expression softened, and for a moment, I thought he was about to say something, but the sound of an approaching cab cut him off.

"Finally," he muttered, waving it down.

The ride back was quiet but not awkward. Rishi insisted on paying the cab driver when we reached my building gate, despite my protests.

"Rishi, I can pay my share—"

"Nope," he said, pulling out his wallet.

I frowned, crossing my arms. "You're impossible, you know that?"

He grinned, stepping out of the cab with me. "I'll take that as a compliment too."

He walked me to the gate, standing just outside as I turned to face him.

"Thanks for today," I said softly. "And for the jacket."

"Anytime," he replied, his voice just as gentle.

For a second, it felt like the world paused around us, the streetlights casting a warm glow over the moment.

"Goodnight, Rishi," I said, stepping back.

"Goodnight, Aarna," he replied, his smile lingering as I turned and walked into the building.

Back in my room, as I placed my award on the desk, I couldn't help but smile. Today had been perfect in so many unexpected ways, and as I curled up in bed with Rishi's jacket still around my shoulders, I realized I wouldn't trade this feeling for anything.

22
SILENT WALLS

RISHI

Something was off.

For the past two days, Aarna had been acting... different. It wasn't anything glaringly obvious, but I knew her well enough to notice the shift. Her texts were shorter, her tone colder, and at school, she avoided me like I was invisible.

At first, I thought she was just busy, maybe stressed about something. But now? Now it felt deliberate.

I tapped my pen against the desk, staring blankly at my unfinished homework. My phone sat beside me, the screen dark. I had sent her a simple "Hey, all good?" hours ago, but there was still no reply.

This wasn't like her.

The next day at school, I caught her by her locker before class.

"Aarna," I called out, my voice casual but firm enough to make her stop.

She hesitated for a moment, then turned around, her expression unreadable.

"Hey," I said, trying to sound normal. "Everything okay? You've been... distant."

"I'm fine," she said curtly, her eyes darting away.

"That's it?" I asked, leaning against the lockers. "Just 'fine'? Did I do something?"

She sighed, slamming her locker shut. "No, Rishi. You didn't. I just have a lot on my mind, okay?"

Before I could say anything else, she walked away, leaving me standing there, confused and frustrated.

The rest of the day was no better. In class, she sat as far from me as possible. At lunch, she chose a spot with her other friends, deliberately avoiding our usual table. Even when we crossed paths in the hallway, she barely acknowledged me.

By the time school ended, my patience was wearing thin. I couldn't take the silence anymore.

That evening, I paced around my room, debating whether to call her. Was I overthinking this? Maybe she really was just stressed. But what if something else was going on—something she wasn't telling me?

Finally, I grabbed my phone and dialed her number. It rang and rang, but she didn't pick up.

I tried again.

And again.

On the fourth attempt, she finally answered.

"What?" she said, her tone clipped.

"Aarna, seriously? What's going on with you?"

"I told you, Rishi," she said with a sigh. "I'm fine."

"You're not," I shot back. "You've been ignoring me for days. Did I do something wrong? Just tell me!"

There was a long pause on the other end of the line.

"It's not about you," she said finally, her voice softer now.

"Then what is it?" I asked, my frustration melting into concern.

"I... I don't know how to explain it," she admitted. "I just need some space right now, okay?"

"Space?" I repeated, the word feeling foreign in my mouth. "Aarna, if something's bothering you, you can talk to me. You know that, right?"

"I know," she said quietly. "I just... I can't right now."

Before I could respond, she hung up.

That night, as I lay in bed staring at the ceiling, her words echoed in my mind. "I just need some space."

What did that even mean?

For the first time since we'd confessed our feelings, I felt a strange distance between us—like a wall had sprung up out of nowhere. And no matter how hard I tried, I couldn't figure out why.

23
SECRETS IN INK

———◦♡◦———

AARNA

My diary was my sanctuary.

Late at night, when the house was silent and the world seemed far away, I poured my heart into those pages—every thought, every feeling about Rishi. It wasn't just about him, though. It was where I documented my highs and lows, my dreams, and my fears.

But now, that sanctuary had been invaded.

I sat on my bed, my knees pulled to my chest, staring at the diary lying on the table. It looked harmless, its worn-out cover and dog-eared pages betraying none of the chaos it had caused.

"Aarna, I need to talk to you," Mumma had said earlier that evening, holding the diary in her hand. Her tone was calm, but her eyes... they were sharp, questioning.

My heart sank as she sat me down.

"Is this all true?" she asked, flipping through the pages, her gaze flickering between me and the ink-stained confessions.

I wanted to disappear.

"It's not what you think," I muttered, my voice barely above a whisper.

"Aarna," she said firmly, setting the diary down. "You're too young for this. Do you understand what kind of problems this can cause? Rishi's family and ours are close. We're family friends. What do you think will happen if they find out about... this?"

Her words hit me like a cold slap.

"It's not serious," I tried to explain, though even I wasn't sure if that was true. "We're just—"

"Just what?" she interrupted. "This isn't a movie, Aarna. Life doesn't work that way. You need to stop this... whatever this is. Focus on your studies, on your future."

Her voice softened, but the weight of her words remained. "I know you're smart, and I trust you. But this—this can't go on."

I nodded silently, my throat tight with unshed tears.

The next few days were a blur.

Avoiding Rishi wasn't easy. Everywhere I turned, he seemed to be there—at school, in the hallways, even in my thoughts. And every time I saw him, I felt the sting of guilt. He didn't deserve this. But what choice did I have?

I couldn't let Mumma find another reason to suspect something. And I couldn't risk things becoming complicated between our families.

So, I did what I had to.

I ignored his texts, avoided him at school, and kept our conversations to a minimum. Each time I brushed past him without a word, it felt like a tiny piece of me was breaking.

The year dragged on, but somehow, I kept my focus. I poured everything into my studies, channeling all the confusion and frustration into something productive.

When the final results came out, I wasn't surprised to see my name at the top of the list. It was a small victory, but it felt hollow.

On the first day of the new academic year, I walked into the classroom with a strange mix of nerves and anticipation. Would Rishi still be upset with me? Would things ever go back to the way they were?

As I scanned the room, my eyes landed on him. He was sitting near the window, his head turned slightly as he stared outside.

Our eyes met for a fleeting moment before I quickly looked away.

"Hey, Aarna!" one of my classmates called out, distracting me.

I took my seat, pretending to listen to the chatter around me, but my mind was elsewhere.

The new year had begun, and we were, once again, in the same division.

What that meant for us, I didn't know. But as I glanced at Rishi one more time, I realized one thing: some things are easier to write about in a diary than to face in real life.

24
CROSSING THE LINE

RISHI

It was a strange year.

Aarna and I barely spoke. Not because we fought outright, but because we'd silently drifted apart. And as much as I hated it, I couldn't shake the anger I felt.

She'd shut me out without a proper explanation, and I'd given up trying to break through her walls. So, instead of waiting around, I moved on—or at least I told myself I did.

That's how Niti came into the picture.

Niti was bright, cheerful, and the kind of person who could make anyone feel important. We started hanging out during group projects, sitting together in class, and soon, she became a constant presence in my life.

I could tell she liked me. The way her eyes lingered a little too long, the way she laughed at jokes that weren't even funny—it was obvious.

And Aarna noticed.

She didn't say anything, of course. But I caught her looking a few times, her expression unreadable. It wasn't the kind of attention I wanted from her, though. I wanted the Aarna who'd sneak away to call me on the landline, who'd laugh at my stupid impressions, who'd... care.

But instead, I got silence.

"

Then came Tanuj.

When I heard he'd asked Aarna out, I felt like a live wire had been set off in my chest. Tanuj? Of all people? The guy was loud, obnoxious, and had a habit of bragging about things that weren't even true.

What annoyed me even more was that Aarna didn't seem to mind his attention.

The jealousy bubbled over before I could stop it. If she didn't care, then why should I? So, I started leaning into Niti's attention a little more—laughing louder, sitting closer, making sure Aarna noticed.

And she did.

There were moments when our eyes would meet across the classroom, and I'd see something flicker in her gaze. Was it hurt? Anger? Whatever it was, I told myself I didn't care.

One afternoon, I was sitting in my room, flipping through my sketchbook, when my phone buzzed.

I glanced at the screen. It was Aarna.

For a second, I debated letting it ring. What could she possibly want after all this time? But curiosity won out, and I picked up.

"Hello?"

"Rishi?" Her voice was tentative, almost hesitant.

"Yeah?" I said, keeping my tone neutral.

"Um... I need a favor," she said quickly. "I was at the inter-house wall painting competition today, and I missed class. I tried calling a few people to get the notes, but no one's picking up. Can you help?"

I leaned back in my chair, trying to keep my emotions in check. "You've got other friends, Aarna. Why not ask them?"

"I tried," she admitted. "But... I thought maybe you'd have them."

I sighed. "Fine. What subject?"

"History," she said, relief evident in her voice. "Thanks, Rishi."

"Don't worry about it," I muttered.

When I hung up, I stared at my phone, a mixture of emotions swirling inside me. It had been months since we'd had a proper conversation, and now she was calling me for something as mundane as class notes.

But for some reason, I couldn't stop the small smile tugging at my lips.

75

25

IT'S ALWAYS BEEN YOU

AARNA

Borrowing someone else's phone to message a boy wasn't exactly how I'd pictured my day. But desperate times call for desperate measures, right?

After the wall painting competition, I'd felt like I owed Rishi a proper thank-you. But with no phone of my own, I had to get creative. I remembered our helper Ravi had left his phone charging on the kitchen counter. I hesitated for a moment—what if he noticed? What if he asked questions?

But then I remembered Rishi's number, the digits etched into my mind like a reflex. It wasn't the first time I'd thought about calling him, but this was the first time I acted on it.

I quickly typed, "Thanks for the notes :)", and hit send.

A minute passed. Then another.

I checked the message status—seen. But no reply.

By the time Ravi returned, I was fuming. How dare he ignore me after everything? I paced around my room, debating whether to let it go or call him and give him a piece of my mind.

Clearly, I chose the latter.

The phone rang twice before he picked up. "Hello?"

"Really, Rishi?" I snapped.

"Aarna?" He sounded surprised. "How are you calling me?"

"Doesn't matter. What does matter is how you saw my message and didn't bother to reply!"

There was a pause. "I... I didn't think it needed a reply. You just said thanks."

"Wow," I said, my voice dripping with sarcasm. "Guess I'm not important enough for a reply now that Niti's around."

"What are you talking about?" he asked, genuinely confused.

"Oh, come on, Rishi," I said, my temper flaring. "You think I don't see the way you two are? Of course, now that Niti's in the picture, who's Aarna anyway?"

He was silent for a moment. Then, softly, he said, "Aarna, stop."

I wasn't expecting that.

"I'm not going to lie to you," he continued. "I did have a little crush on Niti. She's sweet, and... I don't know, it just happened. But no one—not her, not anyone—can ever take your place."

I felt my breath catch in my throat.

"I still have feelings for you," he admitted, his voice steady. "I always have."

I didn't know what to say. Part of me wanted to smile, another part wanted to cry, and yet another part was just mad at myself for even caring this much.

"What about you?" he asked suddenly. "Do you... have feelings for Tanuj?"

My face burned. "What? No!" I stammered, feeling caught off guard.

"Then why did you—"

I didn't let him finish. In a rush of shyness, I hung up the phone. My heart was racing, my cheeks flushed.

A few minutes later, I picked up the phone again, my hands trembling slightly as I typed:

"It's always gonna be you."

I stared at the message for a long time before pressing send.

I could only do all of this as I was alone at home that day, my mom was admitted in the hospital for her legament air surgery and there was nobody to ask me questions, but I had to return the phone to my helper so I deleted the chats, blocked his contact so that he wouldn't come to know and i called his phone number by my landline, I just wasn't scared anymore and I didn't want too lose Rishi over any Niti ever again!

26
NOVELLA

RISHI

Art class had been a chaotic blur of canvases, brushes, and an animated art teacher, Mr. D'Souza, passionately announcing the upcoming "Novella" competition at St. Mary's High School. It wasn't just a regular art contest—it was an inter-school event with a reputation for showcasing the best talent in the city.

As soon as he mentioned it, I raised my hand to participate. Painting was my escape, the one place I could express everything I couldn't put into words.

Mr. D'Souza scanned the class. "Rishi, excellent choice. Anyone else?"

Aarna sat in the corner, doodling on the edge of her notebook. Mr. D'Souza's gaze landed on her. "Aarna, you've got potential. You should join."

She looked startled but nodded hesitantly. I hid a smile; her artwork was incredible, and I couldn't wait to see what she'd create.

"Raj, Dhriti, Krisha—you're all joining too," Mr. D'Souza continued, scribbling names on his clipboard as though it was non-negotiable.

When the final list was announced, my name was right alongside Aarna's. I glanced at her, and our eyes met for a fleeting second. She gave me a half-smile, and I couldn't help but feel like this competition was about to become a lot more interesting.

The day of the competition dawned rainy and gray, but it didn't dampen my spirits. As our bus pulled out of the school gates, I settled into my seat next to Raj, while Aarna sat a row ahead with Krisha. The rain streaked the windows, and the rhythmic sound of the wipers added a soothing background score to the chatter around me.

"Are you ready to lose to me today?" Raj teased, elbowing me.

"You wish," I shot back, smirking.

Ahead of us, Aarna was already flipping through her sketchpad. Her focus was intense, and I found myself wondering what she'd come up with.

When we arrived at St. Mary's High School, we were greeted warmly by their staff. They led us to a cozy classroom where we could rest and prepare before the event began. The walls were lined with inspiring quotes and artwork from past competitions, setting the perfect mood.

I pulled out my supplies, the scent of fresh paint and clean brushes calming my nerves. Aarna sat a few tables away, her head bent over her sketchpad. I noticed the way she held her pencil—lightly, as if the ideas flowed effortlessly.

The competition began shortly after. The theme, "The Road Not Taken," sparked a flurry of ideas in my mind. I decided to paint a split path—one side vibrant and filled with life, the other shadowy and desolate. In the middle stood a figure, torn between the two roads, representing the weight of choices.

Across the room, I stole a glance at Aarna's canvas. Her concept was breathtaking: a pair of intertwined hands reaching for separate paths, symbolizing unity amidst divergent choices. It was bold, emotional, and uniquely her.

Hours flew by, and the results were finally announced. Raj surprised everyone by clinching the third prize, and the room erupted in cheers. Neither Aarna nor I won, but the pride on her face as she clapped for Raj was enough to make me forget the sting of losing.

The bus ride home was anything but dull. The rain hadn't let up, and the rhythmic patter against the bus windows seemed to set the beat for our conversations.

"Hey, Raj," I said, nudging him. "Play Blank Space."

Moments later, Taylor Swift's unmistakable voice filled the bus.

"Rishi!" Aarna groaned, whipping around in her seat. "You're impossible!"

"Just spreading some good vibes," I replied with a grin.

She narrowed her eyes, and for a moment, I thought she might throw something at me. Instead, she turned back to Krisha, muttering something under her breath.

A few songs later, her favorite track started playing. Her eyes lit up, and a small smile crept onto her face. She glanced back at me, and I pretended to be absorbed in my phone, though the look she gave me was enough to know she'd figured it out.

By the time we reached school, the rain had turned into a full-blown downpour. I offered to drop Aarna home.

"Rishi, I'll manage—" she began.

"Not happening," I interrupted, flagging down a cab.

The ride was quiet, save for the sound of rain and the occasional honk of distant traffic. When we pulled up to her building, I handed the cab driver the fare before Aarna could protest.

"Rishi!" she started, but I just shook my head.

"Goodnight, Aarna," I said with a grin.

She rolled her eyes but smiled anyway, disappearing into her building. As the cab drove off, I leaned back, feeling a strange warmth despite the cold rain.

27
NEW PATHS

AARNA

The end of the academic year was a bittersweet milestone. I had topped the class again, but it wasn't the result that stayed with me—it was the reality that awaited us after summer.

We all had to make choices. Rishi and I had spent days discussing what we'd pursue. For him, the answer was science. His fascination with physics and mathematics was undeniable. For me, commerce felt like the right path. It was practical, clear, and aligned with my goals.

But that choice meant one thing: Rishi and I would no longer share the same classroom.

The day we submitted our forms, I walked out of the school office feeling oddly hollow. Rishi caught up with me, holding his confirmation slip with a grin. "Guess this is it, huh?"

I nodded, forcing a smile. "We'll still see each other during breaks."

"Of course," he said quickly, as if trying to reassure himself too.

The first week of the new term came with its challenges. Our schedules were different, and the distance between our classrooms felt like a chasm. Rishi seemed to be thriving, though. He had his science gang now—a group of students who shared his passion for equations and experiments. Among them was Poorna.

She had also chosen science, and her enthusiasm for it rivaled Rishi's. They worked on assignments together, stayed late after class for projects, and even laughed over shared jokes. I tried to brush it off, but the pangs of insecurity were hard to ignore.

"Why does it bother you so much?" Simie asked one afternoon. She and Anu had become my closest friends in commerce. Their humor and warmth were a welcome distraction from my spiraling thoughts.

"It doesn't," I replied, though my tone betrayed me.

"It does," Anu teased, nudging my shoulder. "But hey, look at it this way—he's happy, and so are you. You've got us now!"

I laughed despite myself. They were right. Commerce was giving me a sense of identity outside of Rishi, and I cherished the bond I was building with them.

Rishi and I still crossed paths during breaks, but our conversations had shifted. They were lighter, less frequent, and sometimes felt like small talk. I wondered if he noticed the change or if he was too busy with his new world to care.

One evening, as I stared at an unfinished economics assignment, my phone rang. It was Rishi.

"Hey," he said, his voice warm. "How's commerce treating you?"

"Good," I replied. "How's science?"

"Exhausting but fun," he admitted. "You know, Poorna's been helping me with—"

I cut him off, changing the topic. The mention of her name made my stomach twist.

We talked for a few more minutes before hanging up, but something about the conversation stayed with me. Maybe it was the realization that we were growing into different people. Or maybe it was the fear that, no matter how much we cared for each other, life would keep pulling us in separate directions.

But deep down, I knew this was necessary. We both needed to focus on our own paths, even if it meant walking them apart for now.

28
BRUSHSTROKES

RISHI

The invitation had come last week—a formal card with gold-embossed edges inviting my family to a religious function at Aarna's house. Mom had placed it on the dining table, where it stayed until the morning of the event.

"Are you coming with us, or do you have plans to hide in your room all evening?" Mom asked as she packed sweets to bring along.

"I'm coming," I said, trying to sound casual. Truthfully, I wasn't sure how to feel about it. Aarna and I had barely talked recently, and now I'd be at her house with our families.

When we arrived, the house was abuzz with relatives and neighbors. Aarna greeted us at the door, her smile warm but fleeting. She was dressed in a traditional green salwar kameez, her hair pulled back in a neat braid. I couldn't help but notice how effortlessly she carried herself, moving between guests and offering plates of snacks.

"Hi, Rishi," she said when we crossed paths in the living room.

"Hey," I replied, awkwardly shoving my hands into my pockets.

The evening passed in a blur of prayers, hymns, and whispered conversations among the guests. Aarna and I barely exchanged more than a few words, but every time our eyes met, it felt like we were speaking volumes.

A month later, school was abuzz with excitement for the annual fest hosted by William's College. Posters covered every inch of the notice board, announcing events for dance, music, and art. Normally, I would've been the first to sign up, but this year felt different. Between assignments and my growing pile of commitments, I didn't feel like I had the energy for it.

"You're not participating?" Raj asked during lunch, his voice laced with disbelief.

"Nope," I said, shaking my head. "Too much on my plate right now."

Raj gave me a look like I'd just declared the end of the world, but he didn't push further.

Later that day, Aarna caught up with me outside the classroom.

"Why aren't you signing up this year?" she asked, her tone more accusing than curious.

"Just busy," I said with a shrug.

She frowned but didn't say anything more. The next morning, I found out she'd gone to Mr. D'Souza, our art teacher, to insist that I be included.

"Rishi, in my office," Mr. D'Souza called out during the lunch break.

I walked in hesitantly, finding Aarna already there with Simie, who was grinning like she knew something I didn't.

"Why aren't you participating in the fest?" Mr. D'Souza asked, cutting straight to the point.

"I have a lot of assignments, sir," I said, glancing at Aarna, who was suddenly very interested in the posters on his desk.

"Well, I think you should reconsider. We need someone with your skills for the fresco event, and Aarna here believes you're perfect for it."

I raised an eyebrow at her, but she avoided my gaze.

"Simie's already signed up," he continued. "And it'll be a good opportunity for you to showcase your work. Think about it, alright?"

Before I could reply, Aarna chimed in, "You'll regret it if you don't."

Her voice was soft but firm, and something about the way she said it made me cave.

"Fine," I said with a sigh. "I'll do it."

Over the next few weeks, rehearsals became a whirlwind of color, creativity, and chaos. The fresco team worked late after school, turning blank canvases into stories. Simie's precision and Aarna's bold ideas brought a new energy to the group, while I found myself enjoying the process more than I expected.

And though we didn't say it out loud, I knew Aarna and I were finding our rhythm again, one brushstroke at a time.

29
THE PLAN

AARNA

I couldn't stop thinking about Rishi. For weeks, I'd been debating how to tell him what I felt, but every time I thought about confessing, my nerves got the better of me. It wasn't easy when the person you liked had become such a big part of your life.

That's when Simie came up with an idea.

"You should do something indirect," she said while we were sitting in my room. "Something that doesn't require you to say it to his face right away. That way, he gets the message, but you don't have to deal with the awkwardness."

Her suggestion made sense, but I didn't know where to start. "What do you mean?" I asked, curiosity piqued.

Simie leaned in, her eyes sparkling mischievously. "What if I record you saying it and play it for him? Just a casual conversation where I ask you who you like, and you answer honestly. It won't look like a confession—it'll look like best friends chatting."

I hesitated, my heart racing at the thought. "You think that'll work?"

"Of course! Trust me, it'll be perfect."

The next day, right before fresco practice, Simie and I made the recording.

"Okay, Aarna," Simie began, her phone camera pointed at me. "Who do you like?"

I took a deep breath, my cheeks burning. "Rishi," I said softly, my voice barely audible.

When it was done, I felt a mixture of relief and nervousness. It wasn't the same as saying it to Rishi directly, but it was a step closer. "Make sure you play it for him when I'm not around," I reminded Simie.

She gave me a thumbs-up. "Don't worry, it's all under control."

The next rehearsal was at my place. I could barely focus on anything. My palms were sweaty, and my mind was racing. I tried not to let it show as I sat beside Rishi, sketching ideas for our fresco project.

Halfway through practice, I had to go to the kitchen to grab my medication. It was the perfect opportunity for Simie to execute our plan.

When I came back, nothing seemed out of the ordinary—except Rishi. He was unusually quiet, his face slightly flushed, and he wasn't meeting my eyes.

I glanced at Simie, who grinned at me like she'd just won a bet. I felt my stomach twist with both excitement and dread.

"Simie," I whispered later when Rishi wasn't within earshot. "Did you...?"

She nodded. "I played it for him. He didn't say much, but I saw him blush. That's a win, right?"

That night, I lay in bed, replaying every moment of the day. Why hadn't Rishi said anything? I thought he might pull me aside or even tease me about it, but instead, he'd said nothing.

Still, I couldn't ignore the way his cheeks turned pink. Maybe he was too focused on the competition, or maybe he didn't want to rush into anything.

I didn't know what was going on in his mind, but one thing was certain—I'd just taken a huge leap of faith. Now, all I could do was wait.

30

THE DAY OF THE EVENT

RISHI

I couldn't focus on anything. The recording Simie had played for me echoed in my mind on a loop. Rishi. She had said my name so softly, so sincerely, that it didn't feel real.

For months, I had tried to ignore how I felt about her. With everything going on—school, competitions, and... Niti—it was easier to push those feelings aside. But hearing her say it, even indirectly, had cracked the wall I'd carefully built around my emotions.

I needed time. Time to process what I'd just heard. Time to figure out what it all meant. But the day of the event was here, and there was no escaping it.

When I arrived at the venue, my eyes immediately found Aarna. She was standing near the wall we'd been assigned to, talking to Simie and Dhriti. She looked... radiant, even in something as simple as a lilac-colored top and jeans.

"Rishi, over here!" Raj called out, snapping me out of my daze. I joined him, keeping a casual distance from Aarna. My thoughts were a mess, and I wasn't ready to face her yet.

The theme for the wall painting was happiness. After a quick discussion, we decided on a scene of a happy family—a mother, father, and two kids, all holding hands in a lush, green park. It was simple yet meaningful, and everyone agreed it fit the theme perfectly.

As we worked, I noticed Aarna's focus was impeccable, but her hands were covered in paint. The strong smell of the wall paint lingered in the air, and I remembered something—Aarna was allergic to it.

"Aarna," I called out, stepping closer to her. "Are you okay?"

She looked up, her expression unreadable. "Yeah, I'm fine," she said, but her voice betrayed her.

I frowned. "Stop lying."

Her gaze sharpened, and she replied, "I never lie."

I raised an eyebrow, smirking faintly. "Sure, you don't."

Her face flushed, and I knew she understood what I was implying. The recording. She didn't respond, just turned back to the wall and kept painting. I didn't push her further, but a part of me couldn't stop thinking about how stubborn she was—always pretending everything was fine when it clearly wasn't.

The painting turned out better than we had hoped. The colors blended beautifully, and the details we added—like the picnic basket near the family and the flowers in the background—made it come alive. The judges seemed impressed, and though we didn't win, our group left the venue proud of what we'd created.

It was late by the time we packed up. Rain threatened to fall, and the wind had picked up, but we managed to catch a cab. Aarna sat quietly beside me, her hands still smudged with paint.

When we reached her building, I insisted on paying the fare despite her protests. "Go," I said firmly, motioning toward the entrance. She rolled her eyes but gave in, muttering a quick "Thanks" before disappearing inside.

Back home, I couldn't stop thinking about her hands. The paint had been all over them, and knowing her, she probably hadn't even tried to clean it off properly. Without overthinking it, I picked up my phone and sent her a message:

"Use acetone to remove the paint. Don't let it stay on your skin too long—it's not good for you."

Her reply didn't come immediately, but when it did, I could picture her expression as I read it.

"Why do you care so much?"

I stared at the screen for a moment, unsure how to respond. Why did I care so much? Maybe it was because she never took care of herself. Or maybe it was because no matter how much I tried to avoid it, I couldn't help but care about her.

I didn't reply, letting her wonder instead.

31
EXCUSES AND SMILES

AARNA

The days after the Kaleidoscope Art Event were a whirlwind of schoolwork and catching up on assignments, but somehow, Rishi managed to make them anything but ordinary.

It started innocently enough. I was at my desk, flipping through my geography textbook, when my phone buzzed.

Rishi: Hey, do you have the geography notes for Chapter 6? I missed them.

I frowned at the screen, my fingers hesitating over the keys. Rishi? Missing notes? That didn't sound like him. Still, I replied.

Me: You? Missing notes? Since when?

His reply came almost instantly.

Rishi: It happens to the best of us

I rolled my eyes but sent him a picture of the notes anyway.

The next day, it was Hindi.

Rishi: Did you get the meaning of that last poem? The teacher explained it so fast, I barely caught anything.

I almost laughed out loud. Rishi and I were in the same class, and I distinctly remembered him nodding along during the explanation.

Me: Stop pretending, Rishi. You understood it better than I did.

Rishi: I just need a genius like you to confirm.

He wasn't subtle, not in the least, but I didn't mind. Every notification from him brought a smile to my face.

Then came the marks phase.

Rishi: What did you get in math?

Me: 44. You?

Rishi: 41. Not bad, huh?

Me: Yeah, not bad at all for someone who spent the last two periods doodling.

Rishi: Touché. But my doodles are masterpieces, thank you very much.

I chuckled, shaking my head. If his art teacher ever found out he referred to his sketches as "doodles," there'd be trouble.

This went on for days—him texting me about the most random things: asking if I'd finished my science worksheet, wondering if I'd read the English story, even sending pictures of his crooked handwriting and asking if I could decipher it.

One evening, I couldn't help myself.

Me: Are you seriously texting me just to talk?

Rishi: What? No. I have very important academic doubts.

Me: Oh, really?

Rishi: Yep. For example, doubt 1: Why is Aarna so mean to me?

I burst out laughing, startling Mom in the next room.

Me: Because someone's being a drama queen.

Rishi: Rude. Doubt 2: How does Aarna manage to ace every subject? Teach me your ways, oh wise one.

Me: Study. Unlike someone who spends their time coming up with excuses to text me.

There was a pause before his next message.

Rishi: Okay, you caught me.

I stared at the screen, my cheeks warming.

Me: Rishi, you're impossible.

Rishi: And yet, you still reply.

I couldn't argue with that.

Later that night, as I set my phone aside and tried to focus on my books, I realized something. Rishi didn't need excuses to text me.

Not really. And maybe, just maybe, I didn't need excuses to reply either.

32
THREE MAGICAL WORDS

AARNA

I had made up my mind. I was done. Done waiting, done hoping, done dreaming. Rishi had ignored me for too long, and I was tired of being caught in this endless loop of uncertainty. It was time to focus on myself, on my life, on moving forward without the constant ache of unanswered feelings.

But life has a funny way of catching you off guard.

The day started like any other. I went about my routine, shoving all thoughts of Rishi into a corner of my mind where I could pretend they didn't exist. It wasn't easy, but I was trying.

It was late afternoon when my phone buzzed with a notification. I glanced at it absentmindedly, expecting some random message or a group chat ping. Instead, I froze.

"I love you."

Three words. Simple yet powerful. My heart skipped a beat as I stared at the name attached to the message. Rishi.

For a moment, I thought my eyes were deceiving me. Could this really be happening? The words I had been waiting to hear for four years... and now, out of nowhere, they were right in front of me.

I didn't know how to react. My hands trembled as I unlocked my phone, but I didn't open the message. Instead, I called Ariya.

"Get down to the garden now," I said breathlessly, barely giving her time to respond.

Within minutes, I was outside, pacing the wet ground. It was an odd day—it was December, but it was raining. The soft drizzle felt surreal, like the universe itself was mirroring the chaos in my heart.

When Ariya arrived, I couldn't hold it in anymore. I told her everything, showed her the message still sitting in my notifications. She grabbed my phone and read it twice.

"Do you think it's real?" I asked her, my voice barely above a whisper.

Ariya raised an eyebrow. "Could be a prank."

My heart sank at her words, and a pang of doubt crept in. What if she was right? What if this was some elaborate joke? I couldn't take that kind of humiliation, not from Rishi.

I hesitated, then typed out a reply: "Stop messing around, Rishi."

His response came almost instantly.

"I'm serious. If you don't believe me, come to the canteen tomorrow during recess. Alone."

Alone? Yeah, right. There was no way I could face him by myself after all of this. I immediately decided to take Simie with me. I told her everything that night, and as always, she was on my side.

The next day, I could barely sit through my classes. My nerves were a mess, and my heart felt like it was about to jump out of my chest. By the time recess arrived, I was practically dragging Simie to the canteen.

The canteen was buzzing with its usual noise and chatter, but it all faded into the background when I saw Rishi sitting at a corner table with Harsh. He looked up as I entered, his eyes meeting mine.

I walked over, my steps slow and hesitant. Simie stayed a few feet behind, giving us space but still close enough to intervene if I needed her.

Rishi stood up, his expression unreadable. Harsh nudged him, and I could see the faintest hint of a smile tugging at his lips. Then he said it.

"I love you, Aarna."

The words hung in the air, heavier and more real than they had been in the text. My heart raced, my mind blanked, and for a moment, all I could hear was the sound of my own breath.

He was looking at me, waiting, hoping. And in that moment, I realized there was no reason to hold back anymore.

"I love you too, Rishi," I said softly, my voice trembling. "I always have."

His face lit up, and for the first time in a long time, everything felt right.

33
BETTER LATE THAN NEVER

RISHI

I know I was late. Really late. Four years late, to be exact. But I don't regret it. I needed to be sure—not just about Aarna but about myself. I couldn't say those three words until I was absolutely certain that what we had was real, that it wasn't just some fleeting teenage infatuation. And now that I'd finally said it, I felt lighter, freer, as though a weight I didn't even realize I'd been carrying had been lifted.

We were together now, officially. After all the ups and downs, misunderstandings, and silent battles over the years, no one—absolutely no one—could come between us anymore.

Life around us had changed too. Poorna, who used to make Aarna feel so insecure, was now dating Varun, the guy from our physics class who was known for his terrible puns and contagious laughter. Who would've thought? But it worked, and seeing them together felt oddly satisfying. The tension that had once lingered between Aarna and Poorna was now gone. Instead, the four of us had grown closer as friends, and hanging out with them felt easy.

But that wasn't all. Aarna had become best friends with Jay, someone I hadn't expected her to bond with so deeply. Jay was the kind of guy who could make anyone laugh without even trying, and his humor was one of the reasons he got along so well with Aarna. He had recently started dating Saniya, one of Aarna's commerce classmates, and the two of them were inseparable.

Our group had expanded in ways I never imagined. Simie, of course, was still a constant presence. She had this knack for keeping us all grounded, even when things got chaotic. The seven of us—me, Aarna, Poorna, Varun, Jay, Saniya and Simie—had formed a little circle that felt like family. We hung out almost every weekend, whether it was at the café near school, the basketball court, or someone's house.

It was refreshing, this new chapter of our lives. There was no awkwardness, no lingering insecurities. Just laughter, conversations that stretched late into the night, and the comfort of knowing that we all had each other's backs.

Aarna, as usual, was the glue that held us together. Her warmth, her ability to connect with everyone, and her unshakable optimism made her the center of our group. And though I sometimes found myself feeling a tinge of jealousy at how effortlessly she bonded with Jay, I knew deep down that what we had was irreplaceable.

She was mine now, and I was hers.

As I sat with the group one evening, watching Aarna animatedly argue with Jay over which movie to watch, I couldn't help but smile. Life wasn't perfect, but it was ours, and for the first time in years, I felt like I was exactly where I was meant to be.

We had a long road ahead, but I wasn't worried. Whatever challenges came our way, I knew we'd face them together. And that was enough.

34

UNSHAKABLE

AARNA

I should've seen it coming, but I didn't. Maybe I was too caught up in the joy of finally being with Rishi to notice the storm brewing in the distance. It came out of nowhere, blindsiding me in a way I never expected. And the last person I thought would try to tear us apart was Soham.

Soham and I had known each other forever—he was a constant presence in my life since childhood, a close friend who always seemed to have my back. But that day, his words struck a chord of disbelief.

We were sitting on a bench in the school courtyard during lunch, the usual hum of students buzzing around us. I'd noticed Soham acting distant lately, but I assumed it was just life pulling us in different directions.

"Aarna, can I tell you something?" he asked, his voice hesitant.

I looked up from my sandwich, confused by the serious tone in his voice. "Of course. What's wrong?"

He hesitated, then sighed. "It's about Rishi. I don't know if I should even say this, but... I feel like you need to know."

My heart sank. The way he said it made it feel like something terrible was coming. "What about Rishi?"

"He... he's not the guy you think he is," Soham said, not meeting my eyes. "I heard him talking to some guys the other day, and he...

he said some really awful things about you. Stuff I can't even repeat. I'm telling you this because I care about you, and I don't want you to get hurt."

For a moment, I was too stunned to speak. Rishi? Saying bad things about me? It didn't make sense. The Rishi I knew would never do that. But Soham's expression seemed so sincere, so concerned.

"I don't believe you," I said finally, my voice firm. "Rishi would never—"

"Aarna, I'm your friend," Soham interrupted. "I wouldn't lie to you about something like this. Think about it. Has he ever been completely honest with you? Or has he always just told you what you wanted to hear?"

The moment I walked away from Soham, my hands were already shaking as I pulled out my phone. I didn't care if I looked ridiculous, standing in the middle of the hallway, furiously typing Rishi's name into my contacts. I had to know the truth.

The phone rang twice before Rishi answered.

"Hey, Aarna," he said, his voice light and cheerful.

I didn't waste any time. "Rishi, did you say something bad about me to Soham?"

The line went silent for a moment, and then his tone shifted. "What? Aarna, what are you talking about?"

"Soham told me you've been saying things about me behind my back," I said, my voice trembling. "He said you've been... I don't know, making fun of me or something."

There was another pause, but this time, I could hear the anger simmering beneath his words. "Soham said that?"

"Yes."

"Unbelievable." Rishi's voice hardened. "I can't believe this. I thought he was my friend. Aarna, I swear to you, I've never said anything like that. You know me better than that."

And I did. Deep down, I knew Soham's words didn't add up. But hearing Rishi's genuine frustration, his disbelief, erased any lingering doubt.

"I believe you," I whispered. "I just... I didn't know what to think."

"It's okay," Rishi said, his tone softening. "I get why you'd be upset. But Aarna, I promise you, I would never do something like that. Soham... I don't know why he's doing this, but I'll handle it."

After the call, I sat alone in the library, trying to process everything. It hurt to think that Soham, someone I'd trusted for so long, would try to hurt me like this. But it also made me realize just how strong Rishi and I had become.

When I told Rishi what Soham had said, I could hear the betrayal in his voice, the anger that someone he'd considered a friend could stoop so low. But instead of letting it break us, it only made us stronger.

Soham had tried to plant a seed of doubt between us, but all he'd done was reinforce the trust we already had.

The next day, Rishi and I sat together in the canteen, our hands brushing as we reached for the same glass of water. He gave me a small smile, and I couldn't help but smile back.

"Soham?" I asked quietly.

"I talked to him," Rishi said. "I didn't hold back."

"And?"

"He apologized. Said he was just... upset."

I didn't need to ask why Soham had done it. I already knew.

But it didn't matter. Rishi and I had been through too much to let anyone come between us. We weren't perfect, and we didn't have everything figured out, but we had each other. And that was enough.

35

THE BREWING STORM

Rishi

I was halfway through solving a physics problem when my phone rang. Seeing Aarna's name flash on the screen made me smile. Her calls after her commerce classes had become a daily highlight, a small pocket of calm amidst the chaos of assignments and deadlines.

"Hey," I answered, leaning back in my chair. "Done with your accounts war for the day?"

"Rishi…" Her voice sounded strained, hesitant, and immediately, I sat up straighter.

"What happened, Aaru?" I asked, my tone sharper than I intended.

There was a pause on the other end before she said, "It's Soham."

My jaw clenched. I didn't need to hear more to know it wasn't going to be good news. "What about him?"

"He—" she hesitated, and I could practically hear her pacing through the pause. "After class today, I got into a cab to head home, and… Soham got in too."

I shot to my feet, my heart pounding. "He what?"

"I didn't invite him," she added quickly, as if trying to soften the blow. "He just… got in without asking. Said he was going the same way."

My mind raced, anger bubbling just beneath the surface. "And you didn't think to tell me this before?"

"I'm telling you now, aren't I?" she snapped, though her voice still carried that underlying edge of unease. "This isn't the first time, Rishi. I've been noticing him following me. Everywhere. Whether it's after class or when I'm at the library... It's like he's always there."

I gripped the edge of my desk, my knuckles whitening. "He's stalking you?"

"I don't know if I'd call it that," she said, though her tone suggested she wasn't entirely sure herself. "But it's been happening for days now, and today just... freaked me out."

Soham. The name churned like poison in my mind. I'd trusted him. I'd called him a friend. And now, he was overstepping boundaries he had no right to cross.

"Why didn't you tell me this sooner?" I asked again, my voice quieter this time.

"I thought I could handle it," Aarna admitted. "I didn't want to make a big deal out of it. But today... I just—I don't know, Rishi. It felt wrong. I needed to tell you."

"You did the right thing," I said, my voice steady despite the storm brewing inside me. "You don't need to handle this on your own, Aaru. I'll talk to him."

"No!" she said quickly. "Please, don't make it worse."

"How am I making it worse?" I asked, my frustration slipping through. "He's the one who's out of line, not me."

"I know," she said softly. "But I don't want any drama. Just... promise me you won't do anything impulsive, okay?"

I let out a heavy breath, running a hand through my hair. "Fine. But if he tries anything again, I'm not holding back."

After we hung up, I stared at my phone, her words replaying in my mind. I couldn't shake the image of her sitting in that cab, uncomfortable, with Soham invading her space.

The thought made my blood boil.

How dare he?

I paced my room, trying to figure out what to do. I wanted to confront Soham, to make it crystal clear that he needed to back off. But I knew Aarna wouldn't want that. She valued peace over confrontation, and the last thing I wanted was to add to her stress.

Still, one thing was certain—I wasn't going to let this slide.

Soham had crossed a line, and whether he realized it or not, he was about to find out exactly where I stood.

The days that followed Aarna's call were a test of patience I didn't know I possessed. Every time I saw Soham at school, laughing with his friends or casually walking past as if nothing was wrong, it took everything in me not to grab him by the collar and demand answers.

But I'd promised Aarna I wouldn't do anything impulsive, and I intended to keep that promise—for now.

Still, I couldn't ignore the nagging feeling in my chest, the worry that he wasn't done yet. Aarna hadn't mentioned any new incidents since the cab ride, but I could tell from the way she spoke, from the slight hesitation in her voice during our calls, that she was still uneasy.

One afternoon, as I left the science lab, I spotted Soham near the commerce wing. He was standing by the corridor, casually leaning against the wall, but his eyes weren't on the crowd. They were fixed on Aarna as she walked past with Simie.

I froze, watching the scene unfold. Soham didn't move, didn't say anything, but there was something in his expression—a kind of quiet intensity—that set my nerves on edge.

Aarna didn't notice him. Or if she did, she pretended not to. She was laughing at something Simie had said, her head tilted slightly, her smile bright and carefree.

But I saw the way Soham's gaze lingered, the way his eyes followed her even as she disappeared around the corner.

That was it. That was the moment I knew I couldn't stay silent anymore.

That evening, as I sat in my room staring at my textbooks, my phone buzzed. It was Aarna.

"Hey," I answered, my voice strained.

"Hey," she said softly. "How was your day?"

"It was fine," I replied, though my mind was far from the schoolwork I should have been focusing on. "How about you?"

"Same," she said, and I could tell from her tone that she was holding something back.

"What's wrong?" I asked immediately.

She hesitated. "It's nothing."

"Aarna," I pressed, my tone firm.

"It's just... Soham was outside my class again today," she admitted quietly. "He didn't do anything. He just... stood there."

I gritted my teeth. "This is getting out of hand."

"It's fine, Rishi," she said quickly, as if trying to calm me down. "He didn't talk to me or anything. I just... I don't know. I feel like he's always watching."

"That's not fine, Aarna," I said, my voice rising slightly. "He's crossing boundaries, and he knows it."

She sighed. "I just don't want any trouble."

"I get that," I said, trying to keep my tone even. "But you don't have to deal with this alone, okay? I'll handle it."

Over the next few days, I kept an even closer eye on Soham. I noticed how he always seemed to be nearby whenever Aarna was around, how he lingered just a little too long, how his eyes would flicker toward her in a way that made my blood boil.

I didn't say anything to him—not yet. But I was waiting, watching, biding my time.

And then, it happened.

One afternoon, I walked out of the library and saw Soham standing at the main gate, leaning casually against the railing. Aarna was a few feet away, talking to Simie, but her posture was tense, her movements stiff.

I didn't need to ask to know why..

I'd been holding myself back for days, reminding myself that Aarna wanted to handle this without making a scene. But everything changed one afternoon, and the last shred of my patience crumbled into nothing.

It was after school, and I was waiting near the gate to walk Aarna to her cab. I spotted her coming down the corridor with Simie, chatting like usual. But before I could call out to her, Soham appeared from around the corner, heading straight for her.

At first, I thought he'd just walk past. Maybe I'd been overthinking his actions, reading too much into them. But then he stopped right in front of her.

I couldn't hear their conversation from where I stood, but I saw the way Aarna's smile faded, her body stiffening. She took a step back, clearly uncomfortable, but Soham moved closer.

Then it happened—he reached out, brushing his hand against her arm. It wasn't an innocent touch. I could tell from the way Aarna flinched, pulling her arm away as if she'd been burned.

That was it. The thread holding me back snapped.

I was across the courtyard in seconds, pushing through the crowd of students milling about. I didn't care who saw or what they thought.

"Soham!" I barked, my voice loud enough to turn heads.

He looked up, surprised, his hand still lingering too close to Aarna.

"What the hell do you think you're doing?" I demanded, stepping between him and Aarna.

He raised his hands, feigning innocence. "Relax, man. We were just talking."

"Talking?" I repeated, my voice dripping with disbelief. "You think it's okay to make someone uncomfortable while you're 'just talking'?"

"Rishi, it's fine—" Aarna started, but I cut her off.

"No, it's not fine," I said firmly, my eyes locked on Soham. "Not even close."

Soham smirked, his usual cocky attitude on full display. "You're overreacting. I didn't do anything wrong."

I saw red. Without thinking, my hand shot out, landing a sharp slap across his face. The sound echoed across the courtyard, drawing gasps from the students nearby.

Soham stumbled back, his cheek reddening as he glared at me. "What the hell, Rishi?"

"Stay the hell away from her," I said, my voice low but deadly serious. "This is your last warning."

For a moment, he looked like he wanted to fight back, but something in my expression must have stopped him. He muttered something under his breath before turning and walking away, his shoulders tense.

I turned to Aarna, who looked both shocked and relieved. "Are you okay?" I asked, my voice softer now.

She nodded, though her eyes were glossy. "I'm fine. Thank you."

"Let's go," I said, gently placing my hand on her back to guide her away from the crowd that had gathered.

That evening, as I lay in bed, I replayed the incident in my mind. I knew I'd done the right thing, but I also knew this wasn't over. Soham wasn't the type to let things go quietly, and I needed to be ready for whatever came next.

Would you like the next chapter to focus on Rishi processing his emotions after the incident, or should we switch to Aarna's perspective to explore how she feels about everything?

36

STORMS DONT LAST FOREVER

AARNA

My legs felt weak as I walked back home, the weight of what had just happened pressing down on me. I couldn't believe Soham—someone I had known my entire life, someone I trusted—could stoop so low. The way he grabbed my wrist, the unwanted closeness—it made my skin crawl.

But what shocked me even more was the way Rishi reacted. The sound of his slap echoed in my ears, as loud and sharp as the thunderstorm raging inside me. The fury in his eyes as he confronted Soham was unlike anything I had ever seen. He didn't hold back—not in words, not in actions.

When Rishi turned to me after everything, his voice softened. "Are you okay?" he asked. I nodded, unable to form any words. My throat felt dry, and I could feel my heart racing. He walked me home in silence, his presence steady and reassuring, but my thoughts were a mess.

Now, sitting on my bed, I couldn't stop replaying the events in my head. I felt a strange mix of emotions—anger, sadness, and a deep sense of betrayal. How could Soham do this? Had I been blind to his intentions all this time?

My phone buzzed, breaking my thoughts. Rishi.

I hesitated for a moment before picking up. "Hello?"

"Did you get home okay?" His voice was calm, but I could sense the underlying tension.

"Yes," I whispered, my throat tightening.

"Aarna..." he paused, as if searching for the right words. "I don't know what to say. I'm so—"

"Don't," I interrupted, my voice trembling. "You don't need to apologize. This wasn't your fault."

"But I trusted him," Rishi said, his voice heavy with frustration. "I never thought he could... I should have noticed something."

There was a long silence between us. I stared at the ceiling, my chest tight. "I feel so stupid, Rishi. I let him get close. I didn't see it coming."

"Don't you dare blame yourself," he said firmly. "This is on him, not you."

His words made me feel a little lighter, but the weight of the situation still lingered.

"Thank you," I said softly.

"For what?"

"For being there. For standing up for me."

"You don't need to thank me for that," he said. "I'll always stand up for you, Aarna. Always."

And in that moment, even with everything that had just happened, I felt a little safer knowing Rishi was by my side.

The next day at school felt like walking through a battlefield. I wasn't sure what Soham would do after last evening. Part of me dreaded seeing him, but the other part—stronger, louder—refused to let him take away my peace.

Rishi and I decided not to tell anyone about the incident. The fewer people who knew, the better. But my friends were sharp, especially Simie. During lunch, she pulled me aside.

"You've been quiet all day," she said, leaning closer. "What's wrong?"

"Nothing," I replied quickly, stuffing a bite of my sandwich to avoid more questions.

"Aarna." Her tone was firm.

I sighed, lowering my voice. "It's Soham."

Her eyebrows shot up. "What about him?"

I hesitated, not wanting to relive the details. "He's... not who I thought he was. Just... stay away from him, okay?"

Simie stared at me for a long moment, then nodded. "If he's bothering you, I'll keep my distance. But Aarna, if you need help, you have to tell me."

"Thanks, Simie," I said, grateful but not ready to open up further.

The rest of the day, I felt eyes on me. Maybe it was my imagination, but every time I passed Soham in the hallway, I felt the tension crackling in the air. He didn't say anything, didn't even look at me, but his silence was heavier than words.

Rishi, on the other hand, stayed close without hovering. He had his usual banter with Raj and Harsh, but every now and then, I'd catch him glancing in my direction. It was comforting in a way that words couldn't explain.

By the end of the week, word had spread—though not the full story. It seemed Soham had told a few people that Rishi and I were being "unfair" to him. I overheard whispers in the corridors, felt the curious stares during classes.

Simie, however, was my rock. She didn't ask for details again but made sure to steer conversations away from Soham whenever his name came up. And when I couldn't avoid him during group assignments, she stayed by my side, her silent support louder than anything she could have said.

Rishi's support was quieter but just as steady. He'd walk me to the library after school, wait while I finished my notes, and sometimes leave a little doodle or a note in my book when I wasn't looking.

One day, after school, I found a small sketch tucked into my notebook—a simple drawing of a girl standing in the rain, holding an umbrella. Beneath it, in his messy handwriting, he'd written: "Storms don't last forever. Neither will this."

I smiled, clutching the note close. Maybe things weren't perfect, but I had people who cared. And that was enough for now.

37
INNER CONFLICTS

RISHI

I sat in the back row of the classroom, barely listening to the professor droning on about trigonometric identities. The air-conditioning hummed softly, and Poorna was scribbling notes beside me, her handwriting neat and precise as always. Akshat leaned back in his chair, whispering a joke to someone across the aisle. The science batch was a mix of familiarity and new faces, and though the material was demanding, I found myself strangely enjoying it.

Between assignments, extra classes, and group projects, my days had become a blur of numbers and formulas. It wasn't just school anymore—these classes felt like a preview of the future I was aiming for.

But with every new responsibility, I felt the distance growing between Aarna and me. We barely had time to talk anymore. She was busy too, with her commerce subjects, new friends, and endless projects. And yet, I knew it wasn't the same for her. She'd always made time for us, for me.

So, when my phone rang late that evening, her name flashing on the screen, I wasn't surprised.

"Rishi," she said, her voice sharp, a mix of frustration and hurt. "Do you even realize how long it's been since we had a proper conversation?"

I sighed, leaning back against the wall. "Aarna, it's not like I'm doing this on purpose. You know how busy things are right now."

"I get it. You're busy," she snapped. "But am I supposed to just sit here and wait for you to remember I exist?"

"That's not fair," I said, my patience fraying. "You're acting like I'm ignoring you. I'm not! I've got classes, assignments—"

"And I don't?" she interrupted. "Rishi, I'm busy too, but I still try to make time for you. Do you even care?"

The accusation hit me harder than I expected. "Of course I care! But you're being so... clingy right now."

There was a long pause on the other end of the line, and I immediately regretted my words.

"Clingy?" she repeated, her voice quieter now. "Wow, Rishi. That's what you think of me?"

"Aarna, that's not what I meant," I tried to backtrack, but it was too late.

"Good night, Rishi," she said coldly, and the line went dead.

I stared at my phone, a sinking feeling settling in my chest. What had I just done?

I replayed the conversation in my head, wincing at my own tone, my choice of words. This wasn't me. At least, it wasn't the person I wanted to be.

Somewhere along the way, I had let the pressure of everything—classes, expectations, the future—change me. And in the process, I had hurt the one person who had always been there for me, no matter what.

I tossed my phone onto the bed and sat down, running a hand through my hair. This wasn't who I wanted to be, but I didn't know how to fix it.

All I knew was that I couldn't let this become the norm. Not with Aarna. She deserved better.

The days after the call felt heavy, though I buried myself deeper into my routine to avoid thinking about it. Aarna and I had always bounced back from arguments before, but this one felt different—like there was a crack in the foundation we'd built, and neither of us knew how to patch it.

My schedule didn't leave much room for reflection. Mornings were for school, afternoons for assignments, and evenings for extra classes. Poorna and Akshat were always around, making jokes, asking for notes, or discussing topics I barely understood yet. It was easy to lose myself in the rhythm of it all, to pretend everything else was fine.

But it wasn't.

Aarna stopped calling as often. She'd still message sometimes—short texts like "Good luck for class!" or "Hope you're doing okay." I'd reply with a thumbs-up or a "Thanks, you too." The warmth, the familiarity—it was missing, but I didn't know how to bring it back.

Every now and then, I'd catch myself scrolling through our old chats. The endless conversations, the teasing, the "good night" voice notes that had become a ritual. They felt like relics of a time I could barely grasp now.

"Hey, you coming to the café after class?" Akshat's voice snapped me back to the present one evening.

I shrugged. "Yeah, sure."

It was easier to say yes than to sit alone and think.

At the café, Poorna was laughing about something Akshat said, her hand resting lightly on his arm. Everyone seemed so at ease, so comfortable. I couldn't help but notice the absence of a certain lilac top, of Aarna's laughter echoing over everyone else's.

But instead of reaching out to her, I stayed quiet. Maybe it was guilt. Maybe it was pride. Or maybe I just didn't know how to admit that I didn't have the energy to be everything she needed right now.

The next week, I saw her at school during the lunch break. She was sitting with Simie and Anu, her head bent as she scribbled in a notebook. Her hair fell over her face, and for a second, I thought about walking over, asking how she was.

But I didn't.

Instead, I turned back to Akshat and Poorna, who were debating the merits of some math problem. I couldn't bring myself to cross the invisible wall that had formed between Aarna and me.

That evening, she texted:

Aarna: "Hey, can we talk? Just for a bit?"

I stared at the message, my thumb hovering over the screen. What could I even say? That I didn't know how to balance my life anymore? That I was scared I'd mess things up even more?

I locked my phone without replying.

The distance between us grew like a shadow, creeping into every corner of my life. I thought avoiding her would make things easier, that the space would give me clarity. But all it did was leave me feeling hollow.

A week later, Poorna and Akshat planned a group study session at Poorna's house. I went, hoping the distraction would keep my mind off everything. It worked, for a while.

Until I saw her name pop up on my phone again.

Aarna: "I miss us."

I stared at the words, my chest tightening.

I wanted to reply. I wanted to tell her that I missed us too, that I didn't know how to fix what was broken. But instead, I shut my phone off and turned back to Poorna's laughter, pretending the ache inside me didn't exist.

Days turned into weeks, and I found myself spending more time with Poorna. It wasn't intentional at first. We were in the same classes, had the same assignments, and often ended up sitting together during lectures. Akshat was usually with us too, but Poorna and I naturally worked well as a team. She was sharp, quick to understand things, and often pulled me out of my usual overthinking when it came to solving problems.

"Rishi, focus," Poorna said one evening during a group study session. She poked me lightly with her pen. "You've been staring at the same equation for five minutes."

"Maybe because it's unsolvable," I replied dryly, earning a laugh from her.

It was easy being around Poorna. No expectations, no emotional weight—just shared laughs and lighthearted conversations. It felt good, but somewhere deep down, I knew it wasn't fair to Aarna.

I hadn't seen Aarna much outside of the occasional passing glance at school. She was always with Simie and Anu, laughing and talking animatedly. But I caught her looking in my direction a few times. Her eyes would linger, questioning, but I pretended not to notice.

One afternoon during recess, as I was sitting with Poorna and Akshat in the school courtyard, Aarna walked past with her group. She glanced at me briefly, and our eyes met. For a second, I thought she might come over, but instead, she turned away and continued walking.

"Isn't that Aarna?" Poorna asked casually, noticing the moment.

"Yeah," I said, keeping my tone neutral.

Poorna didn't press further, but I could sense her curiosity.

The next week, Aarna and I crossed paths in the library. I was with Poorna, and we were working on a physics project. Aarna was at a nearby table with Simie, but I could feel her gaze on us.

"Poorna, pass me that book," I said, pointing to a thick reference guide. She handed it to me, her fingers brushing mine briefly.

Out of the corner of my eye, I saw Aarna stiffen. She whispered something to Simie, who looked in our direction and frowned.

Later that evening, Aarna texted me:

Aarna: "Busy with Poorna?"

The message was simple, but the undertone was clear.

I stared at the text, unsure how to respond. I didn't want to lie, but I also didn't want to add to the tension already brewing between us.

Me: "We're just working on a project."

She didn't reply.

Poorna and I weren't doing anything wrong, but I couldn't shake the guilt that crept in every time I thought about Aarna. I had grown colder, more distant, and she was noticing.

One evening after class, Poorna and I walked to the bus stop together. We talked about the upcoming exams, laughed about Akshat's silly antics, and for a moment, I felt lighter. But when I got home, I saw a missed call from Aarna.

I didn't call back. Instead, I texted:

Me: "What's up?"

She replied almost immediately:

Aarna: "Nothing. Just wanted to talk."

Her words felt heavy, carrying an unspoken plea. But instead of dialing her number, I turned off my phone and sat in the silence of my room, wondering why I couldn't just fix things between us.

38
THE DATE

It was one of those days when the frustration in my chest wouldn't go away. Rishi and I barely spoke anymore, but every time I saw him, he was with Poorna—laughing, sharing jokes, or sitting close during their study sessions. He always seemed to have time for her. Time he used to have for me.

I couldn't understand why I wasn't enough anymore. I had tried talking to him, dropping hints, even outright telling him how distant he had become. But all I got were half-hearted excuses or cold replies.

That day, as I sat with Simie during lunch, my mind raced. Rishi was a few tables away with Poorna and Akshat, smiling and completely unaware of my turmoil. I clenched my fists, trying to push back the tears threatening to spill.

"Simie, I've had enough," I muttered. "If he can't see me, maybe he needs a little nudge."

Simie raised an eyebrow. "What are you planning?"

I smirked faintly, though my heart wasn't in it. "I'm going to see if he cares. If I can't get his attention, someone else will."

I messaged Soham after school, "Hey, want to check out the new café near school tomorrow?"

It wasn't like me to text him, but I knew he'd say yes. He always did.

Soham replied almost instantly:

"Sure, Aarna! What time?"

When the next day arrived, I dressed with care—casual but put-together. A part of me hated myself for doing this. I didn't even want to go out with Soham. I just hoped Rishi would notice and care enough to say something.

What I didn't expect was Soham's audacity.

I was sitting in the café, sipping on a cold coffee, when Soham excused himself to take a call. Or so I thought. A few minutes later, he came back, grinning like he had won a prize.

"What's that look for?" I asked, narrowing my eyes.

"Oh, nothing," he said, waving me off. But I could sense he was hiding something.

Later that day, I found out exactly what it was.

Soham had gone to Rishi before coming to the café. Simie told me everything.

"Hey, Rishi," Soham had said, leaning casually against the desk where Rishi sat in the library. "Guess what? Your girl and I are headed to that new café near school."

Rishi's pen froze mid-sentence. "Aarna?" he asked, his voice calm but cold.

"Yeah," Soham continued, grinning wickedly. "What do you think we should do after the café? Maybe take her home? I heard nobody's going to be there."

Simie told me Rishi didn't say a word. He stood up, grabbed his bag, and walked out of the library without looking back.

When Simie told me what Soham had said, I was furious. "I didn't tell him to say that!" I exclaimed, pacing in my room.

Simie crossed her arms. "What did you think would happen, Aarna? Soham is obsessed with you. He'll use any chance he gets to make things worse."

I sat down, burying my face in my hands. This wasn't what I wanted. I didn't want Soham. I didn't want games or drama. I just wanted Rishi to look at me the way he used to.

But deep down, I knew I had made a mess. And now, I had to face the consequences.

39

THE CALM

RISHI

I couldn't focus on my work. Soham's words kept echoing in my head, the images of Aarna with him at the café flooding my thoughts. It was my fault, really. I had been distant, cold—ignoring her for Poorna, and now this. What had I expected? That Aarna would wait forever for me to come around?

But when Soham mentioned taking her home... something snapped inside me. I grabbed my jacket and walked out of the library, not caring if I had unfinished assignments or what anyone thought. I needed to see her, to figure out why I felt this burning anger inside me.

I reached the café in less than fifteen minutes. As soon as I walked in, I spotted them—Aarna and Soham, sitting at a table by the window, deep in conversation. Soham was leaning too close to her for my liking, laughing a bit too loudly. Aarna was looking at the menu, clearly uncomfortable, but pretending to enjoy the attention.

My fist clenched around the door handle as I stepped inside.

"Rishi!" Aarna's voice rang out, but she looked surprised. She clearly didn't expect me to show up.

Soham grinned at me, the smirk on his face growing wider. "Hey, Rishi, didn't expect to see you here. You know, Aarna and I were just discussing some stuff."

I didn't look at him. My eyes were locked on Aarna, and the sight of her sitting there, letting Soham get too close, made my chest tighten.

Without a word, I walked over to the table, pulling a chair out and sitting down next to Aarna. I leaned toward her, my voice barely a whisper. "Come with me," I said.

Aarna blinked at me, her eyes wide, but before she could protest or say anything to Soham, I stood up, taking her hand.

"Rishi, wait..." she started, her voice hesitant. But I wasn't having it.

"I'm not waiting," I replied, my tone firm, even though a part of me was still angry at her for letting Soham get too comfortable. I pulled her gently, leading her out of the café, leaving Soham behind with his fake grin.

As we stepped outside, the cool evening air hit my face, but the anger in my chest didn't dissipate. I looked at Aarna, who was silent, her hand still in mine.

She didn't try to pull away, but I could see the confusion in her eyes. "What are you doing, Rishi?" she asked quietly, as we walked down the sidewalk.

I didn't answer right away. Instead, I turned to her, pulling her to a stop. "Why, Aarna?" I asked, my voice softer now, but still hurt. "Why did you go with him? You know I care about you, but you let him... What did you think I was going to do? Just stand back and watch?"

She didn't respond immediately, and I could see she was struggling with her own feelings. "I... I didn't think you'd care anymore. You've been busy with Poorna. I didn't think you had time for me."

Her words stung more than I expected. "I've always had time for you, Aarna," I said, stepping closer, my voice low. "But I know I've been an idiot. I let you slip away because I was too focused on everything else. But Soham—he doesn't get to come between us."

I saw her eyes soften, the realization that I still cared hitting her. She bit her lip, looking away.

"I'm sorry, Rishi," she whispered. "I just—"

"You don't need to apologize," I interrupted, reaching up to gently touch her cheek, turning her face to meet mine. "But if you ever think I don't care about you again, just remember this moment."

I took a deep breath, feeling the weight of the last few weeks lifting off my shoulders. "Let's go home," I said, my voice quieter now, almost defeated. "I'm not letting anyone mess with what we have."

She nodded, her eyes still searching mine, and for the first time in a long while, it felt like we were on the same page again.

We didn't talk much on the way to her place. But when I dropped her off at her gate, I made sure to give her a long, lingering look.

"I love you, Aarna," I whispered, though I wasn't sure if she heard me, but the way she smiled made everything feel right again.

I watched her go inside, and for the first time in days, I felt a sense of peace. Nothing—no one—could tear us apart now.

40
THE FIRST PICTURE

RISHI

The night was alive with the glow of lights and the sound of music. Our school carnival had finally arrived, and everyone was buzzing with excitement. The stalls were crowded with students and teachers alike, laughter ringing through the air. I was with my friends, moving from one game booth to another, but my mind wasn't really on the dart games or ring toss.

That was when I saw her.

Aarna.

She stood near the cotton candy stall, her blue tank top and black skirt swaying slightly in the breeze. Her hoop earrings caught the light, adding a touch of elegance, but what truly captivated me was her smile. She looked... perfect. It was as if the chaos of the carnival dulled for a moment, leaving only her in sharp focus.

Before I knew it, my feet had carried me toward her.

"Hey," I said, trying to sound casual.

Her eyes lit up when she saw me. "Hi! Having fun?"

"Yeah, it's alright," I replied, shoving my hands into my pockets. "What about you?"

"It's great! I've already won two stuffed animals," she said, pointing to the prizes tucked under her arm. "And I'm pretty sure Simie is plotting to win every single one in the stall over there."

I laughed, shaking my head. "Sounds about right."

We stood there for a moment, the comfortable silence filled by the music playing in the background. Suddenly, I realized the song had changed, and my heart sank. Perfect by Ed Sheeran.

My friends—traitors, every single one of them—immediately rushed to the dedication counter, their grins wide and unapologetic.

"From Rishi to Aarna!" one of them shouted loud enough for half the carnival to hear.

I could feel the heat rising to my face as the dedication was announced. Aarna turned to me, her cheeks tinged with pink. "They're impossible," I muttered, scratching the back of my neck.

She laughed softly, her eyes sparkling. "It's a good song."

We listened for a few moments, the lyrics filling the space between us. Neither of us said much, but the unspoken understanding in her gaze made my heart race.

When the song ended, Aarna glanced at me, a shy smile playing on her lips. "Hey, let's click a picture."

"Uh, sure," I said, startled.

It wasn't a big deal—we had both taken plenty of pictures with our friends—but this was the first one we were going to take together. Something about that felt... significant.

We stood side by side, awkwardly close but not touching. I debated for a second whether to put my arm around her but decided against it. She didn't move either, just clasped her hands in front of her.

The flash went off, capturing what was probably one of the most awkward pictures ever. When we looked at it on her phone, we both burst out laughing.

"This is terrible," I said, shaking my head.

"It's kind of perfect," she replied, grinning. "We'll remember this forever."

As the night went on, we didn't take another picture. That one—bad lighting, stiff poses, and all—felt like enough. A strange kind of magic lingered in it, marking the moment as ours.

I walked her back to where Simie and the others were waiting, but the image of her laughing and the feeling of her presence next to me stayed with me long after the carnival lights dimmed.

After the carnival, I messaged her, "This picture just doesn't look right"

"You don't look right", she replied

I grinned and said "Yeah sure, your pictures with Soham and the other guys are alright, but with me eh"

"Jealous? They know how to pose"

Aarna could really act cocky sometimes.

41
THE FIRST DATE

AARNA

The farewell had officially ended, but the buzz in the air lingered. Everyone was scattered around the school, snapping photos, sharing laughs, and making the most of the night. I stood near the stage, watching as people posed in groups, and the thought that had been circling my mind all evening grew louder: I need to ask Rishi on a date.

It wasn't a spur-of-the-moment idea. It had been in my head for days, but I couldn't bring myself to say it. Just the thought of walking up to him and asking made my stomach do somersaults. I was never shy around Rishi, but this felt different.

And so, like any nervous person, I resorted to backup. "Varun!" I called, catching him just as he was about to leave.

"What's up, Aarna?" he asked, slinging his bag over his shoulder.

"I need a favor," I said, glancing around to make sure Rishi wasn't nearby. "Can you call Rishi and ask him to meet me at the canteen? Tell him I want to talk to him."

Varun raised an eyebrow, a teasing grin spreading across his face. "Oho, special meeting? Should I tell him to bring flowers?"

"Varun!" I hissed, smacking his arm lightly. "Just call him, okay?"

He laughed but nodded. "Alright, alright. Anything for you."

I waited at the canteen, my heart pounding. The place was quieter now, with most people heading home or hanging out in the open grounds. When I saw Rishi approaching, dressed in his casual white t-shirt and jeans, a smile already on his face, I felt a rush of warmth—and nerves.

"You called?" he asked, his tone light and teasing.

I took a deep breath, trying to steady my voice. "Yeah, I... I wanted to ask you something."

He tilted his head, curious but patient.

"Do you want to go on a date with me tonight?" I finally blurted out, my voice a little shaky but firm enough to make my intention clear.

For a moment, Rishi just stared at me, his smile widening until it stretched across his face. "Yes," he said, his voice filled with so much joy that I couldn't help but smile back.

That evening, I took him to a rooftop restaurant overlooking the sea. The place was magical, with soft lights casting a warm glow, gentle music playing in the background, and the sound of waves crashing in the distance. A single candle flickered between us as we sat at the table, and Rishi looked around, clearly impressed.

"Aarna, this is... Wow. I didn't know you had a romantic side," he teased, though his voice was soft with emotion.

I laughed, feeling more at ease. "There's a lot you don't know about me, Mr. Attitude."

He raised an eyebrow, leaning forward slightly. "Mr. Attitude? Since when have I been that?"

"Since forever!" I replied, smirking.

Rishi looked genuinely curious now. "And why exactly am I Mr. Attitude? Enlighten me."

"Because you have so much of it!" I said, pretending to sound exasperated. "You walk around like you own the world, with your favorite green shoes and your overconfident smirks. It's like you know you're cool and make sure everyone else knows it too."

He laughed, the sound rich and full of amusement. "So, you're saying I'm cool? Thanks for the compliment."

I rolled my eyes, though I couldn't help but smile. "See? That's the attitude I'm talking about!"

"Well," he said, leaning back in his chair, "I don't hear you complaining too much about it."

I couldn't argue with that, so I just shook my head, laughing along with him.

As the night went on, we talked, laughed, and enjoyed the delicious food. It was perfect—simple yet special. At one point, I reached across the table and took his hand in mine. My eyes welled up with tears, and I spoke from the depths of my heart.

"Every time I look at you, I'm reminded that sometimes, the best parts of life are the ones we never saw coming. You don't know how crazy I am about you, Rishi."

His grip on my hand tightened, and he looked at me with an intensity that made my heart skip a beat. "Aarna, you are the answer I never even knew I was looking for. My day begins and ends with you, and I have never been this crazy about anyone else in my life."

For a moment, the world seemed to fade away, leaving just the two of us. It was a night I knew I'd never forget.

After dinner, we laughed about how we should split the bill, both refusing to let the other pay entirely, until we finally agreed to share it.

When I got home, the night's magic was interrupted by my mom's interrogation. "Where were you till so late?" she asked, her hands on her hips, clearly waiting for a convincing answer.

"With Simie and Anu," I said, keeping my tone casual. Thankfully, I'd already given them a heads-up to cover for me if needed.

Mom squinted at me for a moment but eventually let it go. I slipped into my room, my heart still full from the night's events. I sat on my bed, replaying every moment of the evening, from the way Rishi smiled at me to the way he looked at me as if I was the only person in the world.

It was a night to remember.

42

A NIGHT TO REMEMBER

AARNA

I'd been thinking about this for days now—getting the entire group together for a proper catch-up. Between classes, assignments, and life pulling us in different directions, we barely had time to talk like we used to. So, when I heard about the newly opened restaurant near the mall, it seemed like the perfect opportunity.

"Jay, you're coming, right? No excuses," I had told him over the phone.

"And Saniya, you better not bail last minute!" I added.

By the time everyone confirmed—Rishi, Simie, Poorna, Varun, and the rest—I felt a sense of satisfaction. This was going to be a much-needed evening of laughter and reconnecting.

When the day arrived, I stood in front of my mirror for longer than usual, adjusting the grey dress I'd picked out. It wasn't overly fancy, but I liked how it looked—simple, elegant, and a little different from my usual. As I tied my hair back, I caught myself wondering what Rishi would think. Not that it mattered... or so I told myself.

The restaurant was buzzing when we arrived, and the soft glow of the fairy lights strung across the ceiling gave it a cozy yet lively vibe. I was the first to get there, and soon everyone else started trickling in, laughing and exchanging greetings.

When Rishi walked in, I couldn't help but notice him right away. He wore a crisp white T-shirt, jeans, his favorite green shoes, and that watch he always fiddled with. Something about the way he casually strolled in, greeting everyone with his easy smile, made my chest tighten.

"Hey, Aarna," he said, flashing a grin as he slid into the chair next to me.

"Hi," I managed, hoping my face wasn't giving away too much.

As the conversations picked up, I found myself enjoying the familiar banter, but a part of me was hyperaware of Rishi's presence beside me. At one point, my hand rested on the table, and before I could even process it, Rishi's hand brushed against mine.

I froze.

And then, as if it were the most natural thing in the world, he placed his hand gently over mine. My cheeks burned, and I bit the inside of my cheek to keep from smiling too wide. When I dared to glance at him, he was already looking at me, his expression soft but teasing.

We quickly looked away, but the warmth of his hand stayed, making it impossible to focus on anything else.

When the waiter arrived and asked for our orders, the words tumbled out of our mouths at the exact same time.

"Pasta."

We both paused, looked at each other, and burst out laughing. The group noticed, of course, and Simie immediately jumped in.

"Oh my God, you two!" she said, her voice dripping with mock exasperation.

Dinner went by in a blur of stories, jokes, and delicious food. I found myself stealing glances at Rishi every now and then, my heart doing somersaults each time he caught me.

After we'd eaten, everyone insisted on taking photos outside. We posed under the restaurant's glowing sign, huddled together and laughing as we tried to fit everyone into the frame. Rishi stood next to me, his arm brushing against mine, and I wondered if he could feel the same charge in the air that I did.

Once the photos were done, Jay tapped my shoulder. "Hey, walk with me for a bit?"

"Sure," I said, curious.

We strolled a short distance from the group, the evening breeze cool against my skin. Jay walked with his hands in his pockets, his expression unusually thoughtful.

"It's nice to see everyone together again," he began. "Feels like it's been forever."

"Yeah, it does," I agreed. "Life's just gotten... busy, I guess."

He nodded. "You're doing okay, though? With everything?"

I hesitated for a moment. Jay and I had always shared a straightforward friendship—no unnecessary drama, just honest conversations. "I think so. Some days are harder than others, but I'm managing. What about you?"

"I'm good," he said, but then he gave me a sidelong glance. "You seem... different lately. Happier, maybe?"

My cheeks warmed, and I quickly looked away. "What do you mean?"

He smirked. "You know exactly what I mean. I saw you and Rishi at dinner. You two were practically in your own world."

I opened my mouth to protest, but no words came out. Instead, I just laughed softly and shook my head. "You're imagining things."

"Right," he said, drawing the word out like he didn't believe me for a second. "Just... take care of yourself, okay? And him too. Whatever's going on, it's good to see you smiling like this."

Before I could respond, he added, "Come on, let's head back before they start wondering where we are."

As we walked back, I found myself smiling for reasons I couldn't fully explain. Maybe Jay was right—maybe something really was different.

43

FAREWELL

RISHI

The morning of the farewell was electric, buzzing with excitement and a tinge of nostalgia. The decorations were finally up—streamers, balloons, and banners proclaiming "Farewell, Seniors!"—and the scent of fresh flowers filled the air. After weeks of practice, our science batch's dance performance was ready, and I was leading the group.

I had always loved dancing, but today felt different. Maybe it was the crowd, maybe it was the significance of the day, or maybe it was the fact that Aarna would be watching. My heart raced as I stood behind the curtain, adjusting my outfit for the tenth time, trying to shake off the nerves.

The music started, the curtain rose, and we burst onto the stage. The audience erupted into cheers, their energy fueling my every move. I caught glimpses of familiar faces in the crowd, but my eyes instinctively sought hers. There she was, standing near the front row, her phone in hand, recording our performance with that bright smile I'd come to treasure.

I couldn't help but smile back, even as I moved through the choreography. Each step, spin, and jump was for her.

The applause that followed was deafening, and as I walked off the stage, my friends clapped me on the back, congratulating me. But the moment I stepped behind the curtain, I found myself scanning for Aarna. She was busy preparing for her own performance with the commerce batch, chatting animatedly with Vivan.

Vivan.

My stomach tightened as I watched him laugh at something she said. He was the kind of guy who could light up a room—funny, charming, and always at ease. They'd been close all year, working on submissions together, sharing inside jokes, and today, they were partners in their dance.

I knew I shouldn't feel this way. Aarna and I shared something special, something that went beyond words. But seeing her with Vivan, so effortless and carefree, stirred a wave of insecurity I didn't want to admit to.

The commerce batch's performance began, and I forced myself to focus on the stage. The music swelled, and Aarna and Vivan took their places in the center. They moved in perfect sync, their steps seamless, their chemistry undeniable. My heart clenched as they spun, twirled, and smiled at each other, drawing cheers from the crowd.

I clapped along with everyone else, masking the frustration bubbling inside me.

When their performance ended, the hall erupted in applause, and I watched as Aarna and Vivan exchanged a quick high-five before bowing to the audience. She looked radiant, her face flushed with excitement, and I hated myself for letting jealousy overshadow how proud I was of her.

The farewell continued with the seniors performing their own set of dances, music, and speeches. Each moment was a bittersweet reminder that this was their last day in school, and soon, it would be ours too.

Then came the fashion show. The seniors strutted down the makeshift runway, showing off their style and confidence, earning cheers and laughter from everyone. Prizes were handed out, and as I watched them receive their awards, it hit me like a ton of bricks—our time here was running out.

I leaned against the wall near the back of the hall, away from the noise, trying to process the emotions swirling inside me. The laughter, the music, the memories of every competition, every late-night practice, every stupid argument—it all came rushing back.

"This is it," I muttered under my breath.

I glanced toward the stage, where Aarna was now taking photos with her batchmates, her laughter ringing out above the crowd. She caught my eye and waved, her smile as bright as ever. For a moment, the jealousy, the insecurities—all of it melted away.

Because at the end of the day, it wasn't about Vivan or anyone else. It was about her. About us. About the fleeting moments we had left in this place we called home.

And I wasn't going to let anything ruin that.

44
UNDER THE CHRISTMAS LIGHTS

RISHI

The Christmas fest was a yearly tradition in our town, and this year felt extra special. Maybe it was the crisp December air, the soft jingling of bells, or the way the streets were lit up like a scene straight out of a fairy tale. I was with the usual group—Jay, Saniya, Simie, Poorna, Varun, and, of course, Aarna.

The fest was held in the Canopy Mall, where rows of wooden stalls sold everything from handmade ornaments to steaming cups of hot cocoa. Strings of fairy lights hung from the trees, casting a golden glow on the crowd. A massive Christmas tree stood in the center, its branches heavy with ornaments, ribbons, and a glowing star at the top. Carolers filled the air with warm harmonies, their voices blending with the faint sound of laughter and the clinking of mugs.

Our group wandered through the fest, stopping at every other stall to admire something or joke around. Aarna was wearing a red sweater and jeans, a Santa hat perched slightly crooked on her head. She looked... enchanting. Her cheeks were pink from the cold, and she had this glow about her, like she belonged in the middle of all this magic.

"You're staring," Jay whispered, nudging me with his elbow.

"Shut up," I muttered, quickly looking away, though I couldn't keep the grin off my face.

We all gathered near the bonfire where they were selling roasted marshmallows. I grabbed a skewer for myself, and just as I was about to bite into it, Aarna stole it right from my hand.

"Hey!" I protested, pretending to be annoyed.

She grinned, popping the marshmallow into her mouth. "Sharing is caring, Mr. Attitude."

I smirked. "Fine. Next time, I'll just roast one for myself and… Poorna."

Her smile faltered just slightly, and I couldn't help but feel a little triumphant. "Don't even think about it," she said, narrowing her eyes.

"Noted," I said with a wink, making her roll her eyes and laugh.

As the night wore on, the crowd began to thin out. Our group had split up to explore different parts of the fest, leaving just me and Aarna wandering together. We walked along the snow-dusted path, the distant sound of carolers creating a serene backdrop.

"Isn't it beautiful?" Aarna said, her voice soft as she looked up at the lights hanging above us.

"It is," I replied, though my eyes weren't on the lights—they were on her.

We reached a quiet corner near the big Christmas tree, where a smaller crowd had gathered to admire its grandeur. It was there, under the glow of the lights and the gentle fall of snow, that Aarna turned to me.

"Rishi," she began, her voice barely above a whisper.

"Yeah?" I asked, stepping closer, my heart pounding in a way that was both thrilling and terrifying.

"I—" She hesitated, her gaze dropping to the ground for a moment before meeting mine again. "I'm really glad we're here tonight."

I smiled. "Me too."

There was a pause, and in that silence, the world seemed to fade away. The laughter and chatter of the fest became a distant hum, and all I could focus on was her.

I don't know who moved first—if it was me, if it was her, or if we both just leaned in at the same time—but before I knew it, our lips met.

The kiss was soft, warm, and perfect, like everything else about that night. Her hands were cold against my jacket, but her touch sent a warmth through me that I couldn't explain.

When we pulled away, she was smiling, her cheeks a deeper shade of pink than before. "Finally," she said with a small laugh.

"Finally?" I repeated, grinning. "Were you waiting for me to make the first move?"

"Maybe," she teased, though the way she bit her lip told me she was telling the truth.

"Next time, just tell me," I said, my voice low as I leaned closer.

She laughed again, shaking her head. "Where's the fun in that?"

As we rejoined the rest of the group, my hand brushed against hers, and this time, I didn't hesitate to take it. The others didn't say anything—though I caught Simie giving us a knowing smile—but I didn't care.

The fest continued around us, but nothing could top that moment. Under the Christmas lights, with Aarna by my side, I knew it was a night I'd never forget.

45
DREAMS AND DILEMMAS

AARNA

The moment I stepped into my room after the fest, I shut the door and leaned against it, letting out a soft sigh. My fingers brushed my lips, and a warm smile crept up as the memory of our first kiss replayed in my mind. Rishi and I... It was surreal.

Canopy Mall was the place where I first fell in love with Rishi at first sight and today at the exact same place, we had our first kiss, it felt like a complete cycle.

I changed into my pajamas, but my mind was miles away, lost in the thought of him. Without overthinking, I grabbed my phone and dialed his number.

He answered almost immediately. "Aarna?"

"Hey," I said, trying to sound normal but failing miserably.

He chuckled softly. "Couldn't stop thinking about it either?"

I bit my lip. "Not even for a second."

"Me neither," he admitted, his voice carrying a warmth that made my heart race. "It was... perfect."

"It was," I agreed. A pause followed, but it wasn't awkward. It was one of those moments where silence held more meaning than words.

Finally, he broke it. "Aarna, I don't want that kiss to just be our first. I want it to be the last too."

His words made my cheeks flush. "You mean that?"

"I do," he said. "You're everything to me."

I smiled so wide it hurt. "I feel the same way."

We talked for what felt like hours—about the fest, how magical the night had been, and how Jay had embarrassed himself again with his ridiculous dance moves near the hot cocoa stall. Just as I was about to say goodbye, I felt a rush of boldness.

"Goodnight, Rishi," I said softly, then added, "Love you."

For a second, there was silence. Then his voice came, steady and warm. "Love you too, Aarna."

Just as I hung up, my bedroom door creaked open. My mom stood there, her expression serious.

"Who were you talking to?" she asked, stepping into the room.

"N-no one," I stammered, slipping my phone under my pillow.

"Don't lie to me," she said firmly. "I heard what you said. Were you talking to Rishi?"

I froze. There was no point denying it. "Yes."

She let out a sigh, sitting down on the edge of my bed. "Aarna, I've told you before. This... this is not right. He's our family friend. If things go wrong, it'll complicate everything."

"Mom, it's not like that," I said, trying to explain. "Rishi and I... we're serious about each other."

"Serious?" she repeated, raising an eyebrow. "You're too young to even understand what that means."

I clenched my fists, trying to keep my voice steady. "We're not letting it affect anything. My studies, his studies—everything is fine."

She looked at me for a long moment before speaking. "Aarna, I know Rishi. He's a good boy. But relationships at this age are tricky. You need to focus on your future. If this distracts you, I won't allow it."

"It won't," I promised, my voice trembling slightly.

She sighed again, standing up. "I'll give this some thought. But you'd better not let me regret it."

As she left the room, I let out a breath I didn't realize I'd been holding. At least she hadn't outright forbidden me this time.

46

THE LINE BETWEEN LOVE AND LIMITS

RISHI

I sat at the dinner table, pushing the last bite of food around my plate. My mind wasn't on the dal or the rice—I barely tasted any of it. I had to talk to Mom. The thought had been gnawing at me since the moment Aarna said "Love you" last night. It wasn't just about the words; it was the way she made me feel, like I had found something irreplaceable. But I knew I couldn't keep this from my mom any longer.

After dinner, I found her in the living room, sitting on the sofa with her magazine. The air around her seemed relaxed, but I knew the calm wouldn't last long once I said what I needed to say.

"Mom, can we talk?" I asked, standing awkwardly at the edge of the room.

She glanced up, smiling warmly. "Of course, Rishi. What's on your mind?"

I took a deep breath and moved closer, sitting on the armrest of the couch. My hands fidgeted, but I forced the words out. "It's about Aarna."

Her smile faltered just a little. "Aarna? What about her?"

"We're... together," I said, my voice steady but cautious. "I care about her a lot."

For a moment, she just stared at me, as if trying to process what I had said. Then, her expression hardened slightly. "Rishi, do you realize what you're saying?"

I nodded. "I do. I've thought about this."

"You're still in school," she said, her tone sharp now. "Relationships can wait. This is the time to focus on your future."

I expected her reaction, but it still stung. "Mom, it's not like that. We're being careful—"

"No buts," she interrupted, standing up and setting her magazine aside. "Your education, your goals—those should be your priorities right now. Not this... distraction."

"She's not a distraction," I said firmly, my voice rising just a little. "Aarna's important to me. She makes me better."

Mom crossed her arms, her face unreadable but her tone cold. "You think that now, but relationships at your age can complicate everything. What happens if this doesn't work out? You'll hurt each other, and it'll strain everything—including our families."

"It's not like that," I said again, frustrated. "We're serious about this, Mom."

Her eyes narrowed. "Serious? Rishi, you're too young to even understand what that means. You may think you're in love, but this is just a phase."

"It's not a phase!" I snapped, the words slipping out louder than I intended.

She raised an eyebrow, clearly unimpressed by my outburst. "Watch your tone, young man. I'm only saying this because I care about you."

I took a deep breath, trying to calm myself. "Mom, I know you're worried. But Aarna isn't just some random person to me. She's... she's different."

"I'm sure she is," Mom said, her voice softening slightly, but not her stance. "But relationships take time, commitment, and maturity—things you should be channeling into your studies. If you're distracted, your future will suffer. Is that what you want?"

"It's not affecting my studies," I argued, though the doubt in her voice made me second-guess myself.

She shook her head, her expression resolute. "Rishi, break it off. That's final."

I froze, the weight of her words sinking in. "You're not even willing to consider this?"

"No," she said firmly. "I won't allow it."

A lump formed in my throat, and my chest tightened. I wanted to scream, to argue, to make her understand how much Aarna meant to me. But the way she looked at me—like this was non-negotiable—made my words die in my throat.

Without another word, I turned and walked to my room, my mind a storm of emotions. How was I supposed to choose between the girl who made my world brighter and the family who had always been my anchor?

As I shut my door, I sank onto my bed, burying my face in my hands. This wasn't going to be easy.

47
BREAKING BARRIERS

———◆♡◆———

AARNA

The sun filtered through the curtains as I sat at my study table, flipping through pages of my commerce textbook. The boards were around the corner, and my schedule was packed, but my mind kept wandering to last night's conversation with Mom.

She had given me the green light to be with Rishi, though she'd made it clear that studies had to come first and that we needed to be responsible. It wasn't perfect, but it was more than I could've hoped for.

Excited, I picked up my phone and typed a quick message to Rishi:

Morning! Guess what? Mom's okay with us! Can't wait to tell you everything.

I hit send, smiling to myself, imagining his reaction. But as the day wore on, the smile faded. Hours passed with no reply. By evening, worry gnawed at me. Rishi wasn't the type to ignore me, not without a reason.

I couldn't focus anymore. I needed to know what was wrong. Grabbing my scarf, I told Mom I was stepping out for a quick walk and headed straight to Rishi's house.

When I reached, I hesitated for a moment before ringing the bell. His mom opened the door, her smile polite but distant. "Aarna, what brings you here?"

"Hi, Aunty," I said, trying to keep my voice steady. "Is Rishi home? I need to talk to him."

She stepped aside to let me in, but her expression gave me the answer before her words did. "He's in his room. But, Aarna, I think you should know... we talked last night. About you and him."

My heart sank. "What do you mean?"

She gestured for me to sit on the couch, her tone soft but firm. "I told him he needs to focus on his studies and that a relationship isn't right for him at this stage. I asked him to end things."

I swallowed hard, the weight of her words hitting me like a punch to the gut. "Aunty, with all due respect, I don't think this is just a phase for either of us. Rishi and I... we've always brought out the best in each other."

Her expression didn't change, but she didn't interrupt, so I kept going. "I understand your concerns. Our studies are important, and we both know that. But being together doesn't mean we'll lose sight of our goals. If anything, we've been each other's support through everything."

She sighed, leaning back. "Aarna, I've known you since you were a little girl. You're bright, focused, and mature. But relationships—especially at your age—can complicate things."

I nodded, choosing my words carefully. "I understand that it might seem like that, but Rishi and I have always been responsible. We've kept our priorities straight. And we're not doing this lightly, Aunty. This means everything to us."

Her eyes softened slightly, and I saw a flicker of uncertainty. "Aarna, it's not that I don't like you. You know how much I care about you. But as a mother, my only concern is his future."

"And I promise you," I said earnestly, leaning forward, "I'd never do anything to jeopardize that. I'll make sure he stays focused, just like he makes sure I do. I respect you and Uncle so much, and I'd never let you down."

For a moment, there was silence. Then she gave me a long, searching look. "You're a very persuasive young lady," she said with a small smile.

I let out a breath I didn't realize I'd been holding. "So... does that mean you're okay with this?"

She sighed again, but this time it felt lighter. "Fine. But on one condition—you both have to promise me you'll focus on your studies first. If I see either of you slipping, this ends immediately."

I nodded eagerly. "We promise. Thank you, Aunty. You don't know how much this means to us."

She called for Rishi, and when he came out, he looked at both of us with a confused expression. "What's going on?"

I grinned at him, my heart swelling with relief. "Your mom's okay with us now."

His eyes widened, darting to her. She nodded with a reluctant smile. "Don't make me regret this, Rishi."

"I won't," he said quickly, his face lighting up.

As we stepped outside together, I couldn't stop smiling. For the first time in days, everything felt right again. We were in this together, and now, the people who mattered most were on our side.

48
LOST CONNECTIONS

RISHI

The last exam paper felt like the world's weight was lifted off my shoulders. The celebrations were short-lived, though, as the grind for Grade 10 started almost immediately. Everyone was serious now; it wasn't just about passing but excelling. And somehow, I ended up in one of the most notorious math and science classes in the city—known for its impossibly high expectations and a teacher who could make the boldest students quake in their shoes.

It wasn't just the challenge of the classes that made my days difficult. I lost my phone.

It happened on a particularly exhausting day. I had hopped into a cab after class, juggling my notebooks and water bottle. Somewhere between fiddling with the bag strap and counting my change, I must have left my phone behind. By the time I realized, the cab was gone.

That small rectangle of glass and metal was my only link to Aarna. And now, it was gone.

Days passed, and I couldn't reach her. It felt strange—not having her voice at the other end of a call or her quick, sarcastic texts lighting up my day. I missed her, and I hated how helpless I felt.

In the meantime, Poorna and I had started talking more. She had switched to my math and science batch this year, leaving behind her old one with Aarna and Simie. It surprised me at first. Poorna had always been a bit distant, more Aarna's acquaintance than mine. But sitting next to someone during hours of torturous equations can create a sort of camaraderie.

She was funny in a sharp, unfiltered way, often whispering biting comments about the teacher's quirks or the impossible pace of the lectures. Slowly, our conversations stretched beyond class—casual chats about submissions, jokes about shared struggles, and even random debates about who should win the cricket match of our school league.

One evening, as I was packing up after class, Poorna asked, "Hey, have you spoken to Aarna recently?"

Her question caught me off guard. "Not for days," I admitted. "I lost my phone."

"Oh," she said, her expression unreadable. "That's unusual. You two are always joined at the hip."

I managed a small smile. "Not this time, I guess."

"Hmm," she said, leaning back against the desk. "You know, she's been quiet too. Simie mentioned it."

That hit me harder than I expected. Was Aarna waiting to hear from me as much as I was from her?

The truth was, Poorna and I were getting close—not in the way I was with Aarna, of course, but still. I couldn't help but notice how easy it was to talk to her, how she always seemed to know when to lighten the mood or when to prod me out of my gloom. But every time I laughed at one of her jokes or felt thankful for her company, there was a nagging voice at the back of my mind, reminding me of the unanswered texts and missed conversations with Aarna.

I promised myself I'd fix things. I didn't know how just yet, but I'd find a way to reconnect with Aarna. I had to.

49

FRACTURED TIES

AARNA

The first few days after Poorna left our classes felt strange. She had been my closest ally in that room, someone I'd laugh with during the most boring lectures, share snacks with, and vent about endless assignments. But when she decided to switch classes, everything shifted.

At first, I told myself it wasn't a big deal. We still hung out during breaks and messaged each other like we always had. But something felt... off. I didn't know if it was the distance or something else, but Poorna seemed distracted, like she was holding something back.

One day, I casually told her, "Hey, now that you're in Rishi's batch, keep an eye on him, will you? He loses things all the time and never asks for help when he needs it."

She smiled faintly and nodded. "Of course. You don't even have to ask."

I believed her.

Days turned into weeks, and things started to unravel. It began with the news that Poorna and Varun had broken up. They had always been that couple—playful, sweet, and seemingly unshakeable. So when Varun came to me one day, looking crushed, I was stunned.

"It's over," he said, his voice heavy.

I frowned. "What happened?"

"Her mom found out about us," he said, running a hand through his hair. "She lost it. Said I wasn't 'good enough' for Poorna and forced her to end it."

"That's ridiculous," I said, anger bubbling up. "Poorna cared about you. She should've stood up for you."

He shook his head. "She didn't even try. Just... ghosted me. Stopped replying, stopped talking. It's like I don't exist anymore."

Hearing that broke something in me. Poorna had always been headstrong, someone I admired for her ability to take on anything. But this? This felt cruel.

I stood by Varun after that. I knew how much he cared for her; he'd told me once, in the middle of a silly group argument, that Poorna was the only person who truly understood him. Seeing him like this—hurt, confused, and angry—was heartbreaking.

Meanwhile, Poorna had disappeared. Not just from Varun's life, but from mine too. No texts, no calls, nothing. I reached out a few times, hoping she'd open up about what was going on, but every message went unanswered.

Simie and Anu noticed it too. "Have you heard from Poorna?" Simie asked one afternoon as we sat in the canteen.

"No," I said quietly. "She's just... gone."

"She's ghosting everyone," Anu added, her tone sharp. "Not just us. Even people in her new batch say she barely talks."

I tried to rationalize it. Maybe she was dealing with more than she could handle. Maybe she needed space. But the truth was, I felt betrayed. Poorna wasn't just my friend—she was someone I thought I could count on, someone I trusted. And now, she'd vanished when I needed her most.

Later that evening, as I sat in my room staring at our old group photos, a mix of emotions swirled within me—anger, sadness, confusion. I missed her, but I couldn't ignore the hurt she'd caused.

For now, all I could do was be there for Varun and focus on the people who still chose to stay.

50
AN UNEXPECTED INVITATION

♡

RISHI

The days leading up to the result day were a blur of nervous energy. Everyone in class was tense, trying to predict how they'd done on the board exams. Poorna and I had been spending a lot of time together, and to my surprise, we'd grown close—closer than I'd ever expected. She was easy to talk to, and even though we joked around a lot, I couldn't help but notice how her presence seemed to distract me from everything else.

But no matter how much time I spent with her, Aarna was never far from my mind. I kept wondering if I'd see her on the day the report cards were handed out.

When the day finally came, I walked into the school hall with a strange mix of anticipation and dread. My mom was with me, smiling confidently like she already knew I'd done well. I scanned the crowd as we waited for the results to be distributed, my eyes darting from one group of parents and students to the next.

But Aarna wasn't there.

I told myself she might've already left or had her report card collected by someone else. Still, the disappointment lingered as I walked up to collect mine.

When I saw the 90% printed on the sheet, I felt a rush of relief. My mom's face lit up with pride, and for once, she didn't say anything about how I could've done better. It was a moment of quiet victory.

That night, I couldn't stop thinking about Aarna. Her birthday was coming up, and I hoped we'd cross paths before then. The thought of not being able to wish her in person made my chest tighten.

In the midst of all this, there was someone else I couldn't ignore. Saanvi.

She was in my English class, and over the past few weeks, we'd been talking more and more. It started with casual exchanges about assignments, but somewhere along the line, I realized I genuinely enjoyed our conversations. She was sharp, witty, and had this effortless charm that was hard to ignore.

And, if I was being honest, I found her attractive.

It was strange, almost disorienting. My feelings for Aarna had always been so strong, so consuming, that the idea of being drawn to someone else had never crossed my mind. But now, every time Saanvi laughed at one of my jokes or leaned in just a little closer during our conversations, I felt something—a spark that I couldn't deny.

I tried to push it aside, telling myself it was nothing, just a fleeting distraction. But the guilt lingered, gnawing at me. How could I even entertain the thought of someone else when Aarna was still the center of my world?

Valentine's Day arrived, and I was lounging in the living room, scrolling through my phone, when my mom's voice called out from the kitchen.

"Rishi, it's for you!"

"For me?" I walked over, confused. She handed me the phone, and as I pressed it to my ear, my heart skipped a beat.

"Hello?"

"Hey, Rishi," Aarna's voice came through, bright and familiar.

"Aarna?" I couldn't hide the surprise in my tone.

"Yes, it's me," she said, a hint of laughter in her voice. "Your mom didn't tell you?"

"No," I said, glancing at my mom, who was pretending not to eavesdrop from the next room. "What's up?"

"I'm inviting you to my birthday lunch," she said, her voice softening slightly. "It's at The Cartel, and I'm expecting you to be there."

Her words caught me off guard, and for a second, I didn't know how to respond. "Oh, uh... of course. I'll be there," I said quickly.

"Good," she said, her smile almost audible. "I'll see you then. Don't be late."

As the call ended, I stood there, the phone still in my hand, a silly grin spreading across my face.

The next day, I found myself in a dilemma. What do you bring someone for their birthday when you've known them forever but can't think of anything meaningful? After much deliberation, I decided to keep it simple. I slipped a thousand-rupee note into an envelope.

"It's practical," I muttered to myself as I sealed the envelope.

When the day of the lunch arrived, I dressed casually but neatly, determined not to make a fool of myself. The Cartel was bustling with people, and as I stepped inside, I spotted Aarna almost instantly.

She was sitting with her friends, laughing at something someone had just said. She looked radiant, her smile lighting up the room. My heart did that annoying fluttering thing again, and I wondered if I'd ever get used to the effect she had on me.

I took a deep breath and walked over, clutching the envelope in my pocket. This was her day, and I was determined to make it special—even if my gift was a little underwhelming.

For now, I let the thoughts of Saanvi drift into the background, where they belonged. Aarna deserved all my attention today, and I was going to make sure she got it.

51

THE WORST BIRTHDAY

AARNA

The lunch was nothing short of magical. The Cartel was buzzing with energy, and the atmosphere was warm and festive. I couldn't help but feel a surge of happiness as I watched everyone laughing, talking, and celebrating. But the moment that stood out most to me was the one when Rishi was beside me, looking like he belonged there, as if nothing could tear us apart.

I had invited him to my birthday lunch, and I was so glad he came. There was something about his presence that made everything feel more complete. When everyone started clicking photos, I stood by him, the camera capturing the perfect moments. We posed together in front of the brightly colored backdrop, surrounded by our friends. I couldn't stop smiling as I looked at him, his smile warm and genuine. It felt right.

But as the photo session continued, I began to feel something inside me shift. There was this nagging feeling, like I was standing on the edge of something, and I had to take the next step. I had to know if he felt the same way.

Once the photos were done, the crowd began to disperse, and I found myself pulling Rishi aside, my heart racing in my chest. This moment felt important.

"Hey," I said quietly, not sure if my voice would carry the weight of what I was about to ask. "Can we talk?"

He looked at me, his eyes softening with concern. "Of course, Aarna. What's up?"

I took a deep breath. "I wanted to ask you something." My palms felt clammy, but I pushed on. "Would you want to go on a date with me sometime?"

Rishi froze. I saw the shift in his expression, a sudden tension in his posture. He avoided my gaze for a moment before looking back at me, his eyes filled with something I couldn't quite place.

"No."

The word hit me like a cold splash of water. I stood there, blinking at him, unable to fully process what he had said. "What?" My voice faltered.

"I—there's someone else."

My stomach twisted, a mix of confusion and hurt flooding me. "Someone else?" I repeated, my voice barely a whisper. "Who?"

He didn't answer immediately. He just looked down, his face clouded with something I couldn't read. The silence stretched between us, and I felt the weight of it, thick and suffocating.

"Who is it, Rishi?" I asked again, my voice trembling now. I couldn't understand why he wasn't telling me more.

But still, he didn't respond. The silence hung heavier, and I began to feel a tightness in my chest. What did it mean? Was there someone else, someone he cared more about than me? Why had he never told me about her?

"Aarna," he finally said, his voice soft. "I never meant for this to happen."

I swallowed hard, trying to hold myself together, but the tears were already beginning to well up in my eyes. I wasn't sure what hurt more—the fact that he didn't want to date me, or the fact that he was keeping someone else a secret.

I turned away from him, not trusting myself to speak. The pain was overwhelming, and I couldn't hold it in any longer. I needed to get away, to breathe, to process what had just happened.

But the tears came anyway, running down my face as I walked away from him. I didn't care who saw. I couldn't stop them.

Rishi called after me, but I didn't stop. His voice sounded distant, as though he was calling from another world. I made my way to a quiet corner, away from the crowd, and slid down the wall, hugging my knees to my chest. The weight of everything—the confusion, the hurt, the unanswered questions—crushed me all at once.

Why hadn't he told me about this "someone else"? Why had he kept it from me when I had told him everything?

I realized then that no matter how much I cared about him, I couldn't make him choose me if there was someone else. And that thought, that final realization, was what hurt the most.

52
BROKEN PROMISES

RISHI

The sound of laughter and clinking glasses filled the air, but all I could focus on was the sight of Aarna in the corner, her shoulders shaking as Jay and Saniya sat beside her, trying to console her. Her face was turned away from me, but I could tell she was crying. On her birthday.

And I was the reason.

A lump formed in my throat, the weight of guilt pressing down on me harder with each passing second. What had I done? I thought I was doing the right thing by being honest, by not leading her on when my feelings were so tangled, but seeing her like this made it clear—honesty didn't make the hurt any less.

I wanted to go to her, to say something—anything—that might ease the pain. But my feet felt glued to the floor, as if the gravity of my mistakes was holding me back. That's when Kaina, her sister, appeared in front of me.

Her face was stern, her voice low but piercing. "You promised me, Rishi."

Her words hit me like a punch to the gut. I had promised her.

But here I was, the source of her tears, breaking the one promise I had vowed to keep.

"I—" I started, but the words caught in my throat. What could I even say? That I didn't mean to hurt her? That I was confused? None of it would matter now.

Kaina shook her head, her disappointment cutting deeper than anything she could've said. She didn't wait for me to stumble through an excuse. She just walked away, leaving me standing there, feeling like the worst person in the world.

A few moments later, Aarna approached me. Her eyes were red, her cheeks streaked with tears, but she held herself with a quiet strength that made my chest ache.

"I still like you, Rishi," she said, her voice soft but steady.

I felt my heart shatter into a thousand pieces. "I know," I whispered.

For a moment, she just looked at me, as if searching for something in my eyes. Then, without warning, she leaned in and pressed a kiss to my cheek.

It wasn't a kiss filled with hope or longing. It was a goodbye.

Before I could say anything, she turned and walked away. I stood there, frozen, as she disappeared into the crowd. My legs finally moved when I saw her heading toward the car waiting for her outside.

"Aarna!" I called out, running after her.

She was already inside when I reached the car. The door shut, and the window was rolled up, but I didn't stop. I knocked on the glass, desperate for her to hear me.

"I'm sorry!" I shouted, my voice cracking. "I'm so sorry, Aarna!"

She didn't look at me. Whether it was because she didn't hear me or because she chose not to, I didn't know. The car started moving, and I jogged alongside it for a few steps before finally stopping, watching helplessly as it drove away.

She was too hurt to reply, and I didn't blame her.

I stood there on the side of the road, the sounds of the party fading into the background. The guilt, the confusion, the regret—it all weighed down on me like a storm I couldn't escape.

For the first time, I truly realized what I had done. I had hurt the one person who had always stood by me, who had believed in me, even when I didn't deserve it.

And I wasn't sure if I'd ever forgive myself for that.

53
HAPPY BIRTHDAY TO ME

AARNA

As the car pulled up to our building, I quickly wiped away the remnants of my tears and practiced a smile in the reflection of the window. It was a poor attempt, but it would have to do. My parents didn't need to know. Not tonight.

The door opened, and I stepped out, taking a deep breath before heading upstairs. Inside, the familiar warmth of home greeted me. My mom was in the kitchen setting up the cake, and Dad was arranging the chairs in the living room for the small family celebration.

"There's the birthday girl!" Mom exclaimed, her face lighting up as she saw me.

"Finally, we can cut the cake!" Dad added, grinning as he waved me over.

I plastered on my best smile and nodded. "Yes, let's do it!"

We gathered around the table, the room glowing with the soft light of the candles. My little sister Kaina was already singing the birthday song before anyone else could start. Her enthusiasm made everyone laugh, and for a moment, I felt lighter.

I closed my eyes and made a wish before blowing out the candles. The room erupted into cheers, and for a fleeting moment, I let myself enjoy it. The sweet taste of the cake distracted me, and everyone's laughter filled the air.

But the weight in my chest never left.

After the cake-cutting and a few photos, I turned to my parents with a small smile. "I'm a bit tired. It's been a long day. Can I go to bed?"

Mom looked at me with concern. "Are you okay, Aarna? Did something happen?"

"No, nothing," I lied, shaking my head. "It was a wonderful day. I just need some rest."

She nodded, thankfully not pressing further. "Alright, sweetheart. Goodnight."

I climbed the stairs to my room, my legs feeling heavier with each step. Once inside, I locked the door and sat on my bed, staring at the blank pages of my diary on the nightstand.

I hadn't written in it in so long. There hadn't been a need to—not when Rishi had been my living, breathing diary. But now...

I grabbed a pen and opened it, flipping to the next blank page. My hand trembled as I wrote the date at the top.

14-03-20

Dear diary,

I know I've not written in you for a long time. That was because I found my human diary—Rishi.

The words blurred as tears filled my eyes, but I forced myself to keep going.

He was the one I could tell everything to. He knew my secrets, my dreams, my fears... He was my everything. From the time we were kids to now, he's been my constant. My person. The one I thought I'd have forever.

And today, he's gone.

I paused, the pen hovering over the page as the pain of those words hit me again.

I feel devastated. Betrayed. And so utterly alone. It's my birthday, and all I can think about is how everything has fallen apart.

I wiped my eyes, my tears smudging the ink as I wrote the next line.

A very happy birthday to me.

I closed the diary and hugged it tightly to my chest, as if it could somehow hold me together when everything else was breaking apart.

Lying back on my bed, I stared at the ceiling, replaying the events of the day over and over. The laughter, the cake, the photos—it all felt so hollow now.

All I wanted was for this day to end. For the ache in my chest to fade. But deep down, I knew it wouldn't.

Not for a long time.

I called up Ariya and told her to get down. All i needed to do was rant, shout and take all of my emotions out me so i did the exact same.

54
UP ALL NIGHT

RISHI

It had been a month since I lost my phone. A month of silence. A month of avoiding thoughts I didn't want to confront.

After what happened on Aarna's birthday, I thought it was best to give her space—to let her heal without me complicating things further. But each day without talking to her felt heavier than the last.

When I finally got a new phone, the first number I saved was hers. The first message I typed was simple:

Hey.

I stared at the screen, the blue send button taunting me. Would she even reply? Did she still hate me for ruining her birthday? I didn't even know if she forgave me and to be honest i knew i didn't deserve to be forgiven.

I hit send before I could overthink and tossed the phone aside, pretending not to care. But the truth was, I couldn't stop glancing at it every few minutes.

Hours passed with no reply. By the time the clock struck 11 PM, I had given up hope. Maybe she had moved on, and I was just a ghost from her past she didn't want to revisit.

Then, a soft buzz lit up my screen.

Hi. New phone?

I couldn't help but smile. Trust Aarna to skip straight to the point. I typed back quickly:

Yeah. Finally replaced the old one. How are you?

There was a pause, and for a moment, I thought she wouldn't reply. But then another buzz:

I'm okay. You?

Surviving.

Same.

It was a small exchange, but somehow, it felt like the dam had broken. One text led to another, and before I knew it, we were talking like we used to—about everything and nothing all at once.

We talked about school, her exams, and how weird things had been lately. I told her about my new math classes and how strict they were, and she teased me about struggling with equations again.

Didn't I already tutor you for this once? she texted, adding a laughing emoji.

Yeah, but I have a terrible teacher now, I replied. I miss my old one.

Should've thought of that before ditching her, she shot back, and I could almost hear her voice saying it.

Our conversation drifted to lighter topics—movies, songs, random memes we sent back and forth. It felt so natural, so easy, like nothing had ever changed between us.

The clock read 3:00 AM, and we were still texting. It didn't feel like hours had passed—it felt like I was catching up on lost time with Aarna.

How are you still awake? I teased.

You started it, she shot back. Besides, I'm wide awake now. This is your fault, Rishi.

I smiled. It felt like old times again, and for a moment, I forgot all the distance and complications that had come between us.

The conversation turned to everything and nothing. She told me about her latest obsession with baking and how she almost set her kitchen on fire. I laughed, telling her about a disastrous science experiment I'd messed up in class.

But as the night stretched on, I could sense something shifting in her tone. Her replies grew slower, more thoughtful. And then it came:

Rishi, can I ask you something?

Of course.

There was a pause before her next text appeared.

The girl... the one you mentioned on my birthday. Was it Poorna?

I froze. I knew this question would come up sooner or later. A part of me had hoped she wouldn't bring it up tonight—tonight when things felt light and easy.

No, I replied simply.

Then who?

I hesitated, my fingers hovering over the keyboard. But I owed her the truth. If there was one thing I'd learned from everything that happened, it was that Aarna deserved honesty.

Saanvi, I finally typed.

There was a long silence. I stared at the screen, wondering if I had made things worse. Then her reply came, and it broke my heart a little.

Oh.

It wasn't real, Aarna, I wrote quickly. She was... an illusion. I thought I liked her, but it wasn't what I thought it was.

An illusion? she asked, her words sharp.

Yeah, I replied. Because even when I was with her, my thoughts kept drifting back to you. No one else ever made me feel the way you do. No one else ever mattered the way you do.

I waited, my chest tightening with every second that passed without a reply. Finally, her next message appeared.

Then why did you hurt me? Why didn't you just tell me?

Because I was confused, Aarna. I didn't want to hurt you, but in trying to figure out my own feelings, I messed everything up. I'm sorry.

You really mean that?

I do. Aarna... it was always you. It's always going to be you.

The screen stayed quiet for a moment, and then her reply came, simple yet powerful:

Okay.

It wasn't a grand declaration, but it didn't need to be. It was enough to make my chest feel lighter.

We continued talking, the conversation taking a softer, easier turn. By the time the first rays of sunlight seeped through my window, I realized it was 7 AM.

We've been up all night, I typed, laughing.

You're impossible, Rishi, she replied, adding a rolling-eyes emoji.

I'm glad we talked.

Me too, she wrote. Then, after a pause: Good morning, Rishi.

I grinned.

Good morning, Aarna.

55

A WORLD ON PAUSE

AARNA

March 2020. The world felt like it had come to a halt, and so had life as we knew it.

School was shut indefinitely, and the reality of the pandemic began to sink in. Masks, sanitizers, and social distancing became the norm, but nothing could replace the emptiness of not walking into our classrooms one last time. This was supposed to be our year—the final chapter of our school lives—and now it felt stolen.

I missed the smell of chalk dust, the hum of our chaotic classroom, and even the dreaded morning assemblies. Most of all, I missed the little moments—Rishi's stupid jokes, sharing notes, sneaking glances across the room during lectures.

Rishi and I texted often during the lockdown. It wasn't like before, but it wasn't distant either. It was... something.

One evening, I was sitting at my desk, pretending to study but really scrolling through Instagram when his message popped up.

"Hey, can we talk?"

"We are talking, aren't we?" I replied, trying to keep it light.

"I mean seriously, Aarna."

I sighed, putting my phone down for a moment before picking it back up. "What's up?"

"I've been thinking... we should get back together."

The words hung there on the screen, staring back at me. I felt my heart skip a beat, but then it tightened.

"Rishi, I don't think that's a good idea right now," I typed back, hesitating over each word.

"Why not?"

I took a deep breath, trying to organize the storm of thoughts in my head.

"Because... I don't trust you the way I used to. After everything that happened, I can't just pretend like it didn't hurt."

"I know I messed up," he replied almost instantly. "But I'm sorry, Aarna. I'll do whatever it takes to fix this."

"It's not just about fixing things," I wrote back. "It's about timing. This year is important to me, Rishi. I need to focus on my studies. You know I want to pursue CA after school, right? I can't afford any distractions."

There was a pause before his next message came.

"I don't want to be a distraction. I just... I want to be there for you."

I stared at his words, torn between the warmth they brought and the ache they carried.

"Maybe we should just be friends for now," I typed, my hands trembling slightly. "We can figure the rest out later."

"Friends?" he replied. "And then what?"

"And then... maybe we'll date later. When the time is right."

His reply took longer this time. "Okay. If that's what you want. I'll wait, Aarna."

I felt a lump form in my throat. The sincerity in his words was palpable, but I couldn't let myself be swayed.

"Thank you," I finally replied.

As I set my phone aside, I looked out of the window at the eerily quiet streets. The world was on pause, and so were we.

I didn't know what the future held, but for now, this was enough. I would focus on my dreams, on myself, and maybe—just maybe—when the time was right, things would fall into place.

56

FULL CIRCLE

RISHI

The lockdown had blurred the days into weeks, and weeks into months. But one thing had stayed constant: Aarna. Even if we weren't together, not the way we used to be, she was always there in the background of my life, like the hum of a familiar tune.

This evening was one of those rare moments when I allowed myself to reminisce. My room was dimly lit, a mug of half-drunk coffee on my desk, and my fingers absentmindedly traced the edge of a small wooden box I kept hidden under my bed.

I opened it gently, revealing the little treasures inside. At the top lay the couple bracelet she'd given me last Valentine's Day, simple but meaningful. She had laughed when she handed it to me, saying, "It's cheesy, I know. But this way, we'll match."

I held it up to the light, the faint shine of the metal catching my eye. It still fit perfectly, though I hadn't worn it in a while.

Underneath the bracelet was a stack of memories: the movie ticket from our first date, the dinner bill from that same evening with her scribbled note, "You're paying next time!" on the back. There was her silver hoop earring—the one she thought she lost but I'd found at the base of my car seat—and a pen she'd lent me during a particularly boring lecture.

And then, there was our first awkward photo together. We'd clicked it in the school corridor after losing a bet to Jay and Saniya.

It was blurry and imperfect, but it was us.

I smiled to myself, closing the box. Even after everything, she was still my person.

As if on cue, my phone buzzed. It was Jay.

"Hey, lockdown's opening for a few days. Everyone's meeting at Starbucks tomorrow. Be there!"

I didn't need to think twice. The thought of seeing everyone after so long, of seeing her, sent a jolt of excitement through me.

The next afternoon, I reached Starbucks earlier than everyone else, nervously drumming my fingers on the table. Slowly, one by one, familiar faces walked in: Jay, Saniya, Krisha, and finally, Aarna.

She walked in wearing a simple outfit- jeans and a cropped top, her hair open, looking like the Aarna I had always known—calm, composed, and radiant. She spotted me and smiled, the kind of smile that tugged at memories and promises we had once made.

We all talked, laughed, and caught up as if no time had passed. Jay and Krisha were their usual chaotic selves, and Saniya couldn't stop teasing me about my new haircut. But amidst all the chatter, my eyes often found Aarna's, and she'd smile back, as if to say, I see you.

After the meetup, I offered to drop her home. She agreed with a small nod, and as we stepped out into the golden evening light, it felt like no time had passed.

The drive to her place was filled with comfortable silence and soft laughter. As I pulled up to her building, she looked at me and said, "Thanks for the ride, Rishi."

"Anytime," I replied, smiling.

She stepped out, pausing for a moment before turning back to me. "It's nice, you know... just being friends."

I nodded, though a part of me wanted to say more. But I didn't.

As I watched her walk away, I couldn't help but feel that, even though we had chosen to stay friends for now, this wasn't the end of our story.

It was the same feeling as before—the feeling of belonging, of warmth, of Aarna.

And maybe, just maybe, that was enough for now.

The Tangled Series

The Tangled series begins with Tangled Love, where Aarna and Rishi's journey begins with love, heartbreak, and self-discovery. Book two, Tangled Hearts, is coming soon, and the adventure continues as the characters evolve and face new challenges. Stay tuned for more!

Follow the Author

Stay updated on upcoming books in the Tangled series and beyond. Connect with Aaska on:

Instagram:- @aaska_1403